The Diggings are Silent
and other Australian Stories

by Wendy Evans

Cover image: Wendy J Evans, from the collection of Bob Scott Esq
Author photos: Donna Swan of Swan Photography

The Diggings Are Silent

Copyright: Wendy Evans
Published: 15th March 2014
ISBN: 978-0-9924784-1-4
Print Edition

The Diggings Are Silent

Come pay the grim reaper as life leaves the land.
The seeds of disaster he scatters by hand.
He harvests destruction and famine and fears
And we pay the grim reaper in sorrow and tears.

~

Come pay the grim reaper as life leaves the crops.
His breath blights the praties and the hanging fruit drops.
The wheat's rusty red; barley's black in the ears
And we pay the grim reaper in sorrow and tears.

~

Come pay the grim reaper as life leaves the stock,
As the drought withers all and the pasture is rock.
The carcasses lie and the corpse wool he shears
And we pay the grim reaper in sorrow and tears.

~

Come pay the grim reaper as life leaves the soil
As he mocks at our suffering and scorns years of toil.
His harvest-time comes and his sickness appears
And we pay the grim reaper in sorrow and tears.

~

Come pay the grim reaper when life leaves the heart,
And his servants, the quick and alive, tear apart.
There's little that's left, if the rent's in arrears,
And we pay the grim reaper in sorrow and tears.

~

Come pay the grim reaper as life leaves the earth
And the shadow of death masks the gladness of birth.
He cuts with his scythe and he harvests the years
And we pay the grim reaper in sorrow and tears.

~

I, Sean Patrick Malloy, born Balfearna, County Kerry, 1846, now dying in the Carramine, near Marble Bar, in the East Pilbara, write this record of my life in order that its sweetness and its bitterness shall be witnessed by posterity.

I was brought to Australia by my Uncle Dominic, a sailor turned farmer, who took over the care of our family when my father died of tuberculosis in the grim decade which followed the Great Famine. He saw to our education and discipline and taught me to be not only a man, but a poet, for the art of the shanachie was strong with him.

When my mother decided to remarry he called a family council, mainly to scrape together the fare to Australia. There and then it was decided I too should take the road to fortune. I was a broth of a boy, toughened by hard work and poverty so that I had a man's stature. My young female cousins adored me and called me handsome. They giggled when I smiled at them or squealed with delight when I tickled them in the hay.

Only Clare remained aloof from the nonsense. She was the companion of my quiet moods, and, although she was six years younger than I, there lay between us a strong rapport which knew nothing of age. It was she who bathed my wounds and soothed my injured pride, who listened to my songs and let me kiss her in the meadow flowers. Her hair curled in soft golden waves around her sweet face. I laughed at the pollen on her nose and told her I loved her dearly.

It was all innocence with Clare. Not so with others and it's my belief they sent me off before my budding manhood caused a local scandal! I frequently forgot Clare altogether, but she was often there like a soft shadow in my life. She was the only one of the girls to cry when I left. She put her hands in mine and gazed at me with tear-filled eyes.

"Don't forget me, will you, Sean" she whispered.

"Now how could I forget my Clare," I smiled, suddenly very grown up. "Aren't you me darling and me love? I'll be sending for you one day, mavoureen, and it's me wife you'll be!" Then I kissed her cheek and hugged her tightly.

Such are the promises of youth. It was not sea spray that wet my cheeks as we left harbour, though the taste was just as salty.

Shed a tear for the green hills of Ireland.
Shed a tear for the peat fire's bright flame.
Shed a tear for the friends of your childhood
And the families you won't see again.
For we're sailing, sailing, blow the winds wild.
Sailing far from home, wife and child,
For the winds they blow wild and the winds they blow well,
And we're sailing away to colonial hell.

~

Shed a tear for the song of the skylark,
Though they say that the bellbird sings well.
Now it may have the voice of an angel;
If it can't sing a home song, it's hell.

~

Shed a tear for the oak and the ash tree,

Though the ghost gum is noble, they say.

If green spring and September gold's missing

Then to ashes it can burn away.

~

Shed a tear for the streets of my city,

Though they say Sydney Town's looking fine.

If it's not your home town it's not pretty.

It's the colonists' home. Ireland's mine.

For we're sailing, sailing, blow the winds wild.

Sailing far from home, wife and child,

For the winds they blow wild and the winds they blow well,

And we're sailing away to colonial hell.

~

Some humorist had classed our leaking crate a boat, and it was with prayers of thanksgiving, mainly for a strong stomach, that we landed at Sydney. Sydney then was the hub of the continent, a thriving metropolis in a country with a future. This was the life for me, but it was not there Uncle Dominic had planned to carve out his future, and mine.

We took lodgings in a boarding house near the coaching inns and both set forth on a quest for knowledge. Uncle Dominic talked to travellers, studied the papers and spent much time with weighty tomes in the Library. I studied other mysteries in the compliant arms of the landlady's daughter. Uncle Dominic viewed this liaison with a jaundiced eye. He walked in one night, threw a swag onto my bed and bid me take an early night as the carrier left at dawn.

"You're thinking you're a great man, no doubt, young Sean, but you need a few muscles to round off your education! We're off to the Goldfields, and if we don't make a fortune, at least I'll have the satisfaction of seeing that smug grin wiped off your face!"

He was right on both counts. We never made a fortune, but we always did well enough. We were of the lucky breed who had the elusive ability to smell gold. Hard work was in our nature. We drove shafts and panned and followed the stringers for better or worse. Once we hit reef and sold our claim before it faulted out. We always made enough for a good stake, to send money back to Balfearna, and to live high and mighty in the city until news of a good strike sent us rushing to a fresh field.

It was there, at the diggings, that I became homesick. I would sit on the banks of a muddy creek, patiently panning. The water would cloud and swirl like a crystal ball and pictures of the past would come, mistily, to my mind. I saw places I had loved and my family, and sometimes, unbidden, the sweet oval face of young Clare. I always saw her crowned in golden curls with her eyes full of childish love. Then, if I remembered, I would buy her a trinket from a peddler and send it off with my love and stern words saying she should mind her schooling and become a lady.

In Melbourne one day I saw a doll with a porcelain baby's face and a rag body. I pointed it out to Uncle Dominic as a possible present for Clare. He jeered at me.

"Don't you think she'd be more interested in real babies at her age?" he laughed.

I had never thought of Clare as growing up, and it came as a shock to realise that she was now seventeen. I no longer knew how to write to her and became stiff and embarrassed with words.

Hers remained bright and full of family news and, the information that Patrick O'Brien had been calling on her, courting. I liked Patrick. He was the only son left to the O'Briens and a stocky, reliable lad. It was a good match, but my heart ached.

Goodness knows how much gold I lost that day, for I was lost in thought. I saw Clare clearly then, grown in my mind's eye to the full beauty of womanhood. Words sprang unbidden to my mind and I plucked a melody from the air, as if my song was waiting for the harvest. I copied the verses in fine hand and sent them to my childhood sweetheart.

It was weeks before I shared the words with Uncle Dominic, one night round our campfire as we sang the old songs. Shyly, I told Dominic I had written an air of my own and tentatively sang it to him.

> *"Mirror of gold, what treasures you hold.*
> *Riches for all, so I've been told.*
> *But I look in the water and all I see there*
> *Is the gold of my dreams, of my golden girl's hair."*
>
> ~

"That's just the chorus," I told him and he nodded.

"It has merit," he said softly. "Sing on, Sean, the touch of the shanachie is on you tonight!" He filled his pipe, tamping down the tobacco before lighting it with a stick from the fire. His face was in shadow as I sang out my dream.

> *"I left my sweet love in that green land called home.*
> *In search of a fortune the outback I roam.*
> *Though oceans and mountains may keep us apart*
> *I know I've a place in my golden girl's heart.*
>
> ~
>
> *I first struck it rich as with hard work one must*
> *With three golden nuggets and six bags of dust.*
> *I've got a selection and papers as proof*
> *And another rich claim builds my golden girl's roof.*

~

The last claim I pegged on the gold petered out.
I thought I'd struck rich but the dream came to nowt.
But I'd crushed enough ore to get dust for my aim,
My golden girl's fare was the treasure to claim.

~

So I sit by the water and pan every day
And dream of my golden girl sailing my way,
And the last gold I'll search for, this last precious thing
The bright gold, the bride gold, the gold wedding ring."

~

My voice died away in echoes, fading into silence. Uncle Dominic sat motionless, wrapped in a cloak of thoughts and pipe smoke. He raised his eyes to mine with kindness and sympathy blazing from them, but his words were of rock hard reality.

"Would you be thinking of sending the song to young Clare?" he asked.

I gave him no answer. What could I say? He sat up straighter and pointed his pipe stem at me.

"Would you look around, young Sean. Here we sit, you and I, in a welter of winter mud or summer dust. Our home is a tent, our hearth is two logs and a billy. Our work is grovelling in the belly of the earth. Sure and there's money in the bank, Sean, enough for your dreams and more but you know as well as I, me boy, that the gold is in our blood. Two weeks in the city and it's calling us. It's chasing rainbows, Sean, searching for the crock of gold. When the fever has you it will call you to the very ends of the earth. It's no life for a woman, Sean. Look at yourself in that mirror of gold, my boy, and put away the dreaming! You'd best be reading your mother's last letter, I'm thinking!"

His voice was tired and I looked at him with resentment. Sadly, I realised he was old. Old, shabby, dirty and unkempt, no longer the strong father-figure who had guided my younger days but a man to whom life itself was now a burden.

The letter from my mother carried news which was hard to bear. Clare had received an offer of marriage and her parents had asked would Sean stop writing as it was unsettling for the girl. I thought ruefully of my song travelling towards her and wished it unsent.

By the time it reached her she would be young Mrs Patrick O'Brien. She would smile at my conceit and consign my words to the flames. If my love was at an end so was my luck.

It was a filthy winter. We shivered in the cold, clammy shaft of a new claim, driving after a promising lead, or hunched damply in our tent eating half-cooked meals as the drenching rain beat at our dying fire. The seam was faulted out, the tent blew down in a wild gale and Uncle Dominic took ill with pneumonia and chased his final rainbow to his Maker. I buried him myself and the rain and my tears were as one.

I turned my back on the diggings. Alone for the first time in my life, I felt the need for company and the lights of the city. It doesn't bear telling. I lost my stake, of course, in a wild life of drinking, gambling and carousing. In panic I chased the gold again, but it's never to be found when one has a desperate need. I took my swag and headed where I would.

For years I followed my nose, shearing, fencing, clearing, working at whatever job would give my daily bread. Always my pan and dolly-pot went with me, for the fever still smouldered although banked down by my self-styled 'misfortunes'. I often felt it was my reluctance to gaze into the mirror in my gold pan that lay heaviest on me, for my dreams and my past were locked away in the darkest corner of my mind.

I covered my emptiness with a brash veneer. I was a mad dog in those days, a larrikin of the first order and a scallywag as well, with a reputation with the ladies. I used to sing to them and received much 'mothering' when I gave them snatches of my mirror song. How comforted I felt! Comforted and cheap! But thank God for the barmaids. They gave me what little comfort they could. If the warmth was like a roaring flame which roasts the skin and leaves a chill inside - well, what of that? I was like a wild animal, reluctantly drawn to the brightness of the camp fire - or a moth fluttering dangerously near the flame of a candle.

I carried Nancy in my heart for many a weary mile
And by the campfire late at night recalled her sweetest smile.
She"s mine, I whispered softly, for you know what bushmen are.
Our dreams are wishful thoughts about the girl behind the bar.
Sweethearts, sisters, mothers too, their eyes say, "Let's pretend."
The queen of every bushman"s heart - the barmaid is his friend.

~

At Armidale, in New South Wales, I fell in love with Meg,
Sun-bleached hair and soft blue eyes, and such a shapely leg.
She filled my lonely nights with dreams of home and city life
But, as I rode behind the herds, I knew I"d take no wife.
Sweethearts, sisters, mothers too, their eyes say, "Let's pretend."
The queen of every bushman"s heart - the barmaid is his friend.

~

Oh, have you seen my Kempsey Kate, the red hair just like flame?
I thought of her for two long months, a warm and loving dame,
Until I came to Castlemaine; I set my eyes on Jan,
And I loved both until fair Ruth made me feel twice the man.
Sweethearts, sisters, mothers too, their eyes say, "Let's pretend."

The queen of every bushman"s heart - the barmaid is his friend.

~

The way those barmaids listen to each hope and fear and doubt,
Is loving to the lonely man who drinks until thrown out.
If you must prove that you"re a man, then go where harlots are,
But if you want some love, then that's the girl behind the bar.
Sweethearts, sisters, mothers too, their eyes say, "Let's pretend."
The queen of every bushman"s heart - the barmaid is his friend.

~

Ah, well, I'd sing until the cock crowed, for those women were all the family I now had.

I rarely heard news from home. My mother died two years after Uncle Dominic and my younger brothers and sisters were strangers to me. I saw the newspapers, of course, and read with dismay of the harvest failures in 1879 when the shadow of the great famine fell on Ireland again. This started a chain of events which set my feet on a new path.

My first hint of this came in an exasperated letter from Patrick O'Brien, which had followed me from station to station until it arrived, dog-eared, at Cooper's Creek. Its contents hit me like a sledge hammer. Clare's family had all died in the terrible fevers which had followed the bad years. He said she was living alone and as obstinate as a mule in clover.

"I've been after having her to wife for years," he wrote, "But the very devil's in the woman, Sean, and she swears on the book that she's promised to you. All on account, as I can gather, of some bit of a poem you wrote to her when she was a green girl. Some day, she says, Sean will send her fare and will be waiting there with a farm and her bride ring. Now, give it straight, Sean. If you want her, send for her or write and set her free, for she needs a man to watch for her now she is all alone!"

The devil on it! Is there a worse experience than to be offered the sweetest fruit and know one cannot take it? I was a drover, a rover. No money to speak of and my possessions in my saddlebags. I had nothing to offer her, neither the security of home nor work. The future was as misty as those blue eyes of Clare's which matched the distant hills in Ireland when the soft rains fell. I wrote soft words then of release, begging her to marry Patrick and enjoy the safety of his house, saying that her memory alone was all I wished. I said I was heading west on the great adventure, driving stock from Queensland to the Kimberley. It was in the hands of God as to whether we prospered or perished. I signed my love with a heavy hand and prayed I had done the right thing. I was married to the life of a drover.

The Kimberley is calling and the long drive lies ahead,

To search for open rangelands, for the living, not the dead,

For, hidden in the distant blue, they said that green feed lay

Beyond the mocking desert night, the cruel burning day.

The way to high adventure, the way to unknown country,

The trackless trail, the timeless trail, to far-off Kimberley.

~

The years of drought had scorched the east and bared its very bones.

The waterholes were full of death and all our hopes were stones

Until the rain came thundering down and brought with it the flood.

The bare earth gasped and drowned beneath wild water red like blood.

But Queensland hearts had broken, and so the word was spoken,

To move 'em out and move 'em on, to seek for better land.

~

Big Johnny Durack led the drive; Thylungra's finest stock.

Three thousand miles of hazard through the floods, the heat, the rock.

We waited for the rains ahead, and waterholes to stand

And echo still our curses in that plague-bound desert land.

The way to high adventure, the way to unknown country,

The trackless trail, the timeless trail, to far-off Kimberley.

~

And still they talk in the far north of those who mustered through;

Of Jerry Durack, Kilfoyle, Hayes from Galway and Barcoo.

Six thousand head of stock they drove; it took two years to ride,

And half the cattle perished there, and five good stockmen died.

But Queensland hearts had broken, and so the word was spoken,

To move 'em out and move 'em on, to seek for better land.

~

Now when I see the devil-dust that whirls across the plains

My mind recalls the lowing herds, my back the saddle pains.

Then, in the campfire smoke at night, my ghostly mates appear,

Reliving days along the trail, the laughter and the fear.

The way to high adventure, the way to unknown country,

The trackless trail, the timeless trail, to far-off Kimberley.

~

The story of the drive is history and, although I had time along those weary miles to think of Clare, it was without regrets. I had made a decision and could no longer blame a nameless fate. It seemed as if the new attitude had changed my luck, for we were well-rewarded for the great drive and there was steady work for us in this wild and beautiful country. I had time for fossicking and knew it was worthwhile from pointers given by Michael

Durack, who had found colour in '82. Of course, when Hall struck rich, I was on the spot and well ahead of the rush which followed the declaration of the Kimberley Goldfield in '86.

I was one of the lucky ones for the field never lived up to its promise. I walked tall then, with money jingling in my pockets, and the knowledge there was more to come from a rich alluvial claim I had pegged. I was scarcely prepared for the message which came to me from a new arrival, but an old friend, Archie Clive.

"You'd best be shipping out for Fremantle," he said, grinning widely. "There's a parcel waiting for you in Perth!"

He pressed a grubby envelope into my hand and went to the grog shop for a cool beer from their wet-sacked supplies.

I stood there bemused, staring at Clare's dainty handwriting. And, oh, the news she gave. My mind was spinning and my heart thumping so loudly that I turned my head to see if anyone was listening.

Patrick had been taken with the typhoid and, loving her to the end, and having no family of his own, had left his love and all his land to her. She chided me for my pride, assured me of her continued affection and lack of pride, and told me that she came to me with Patrick's blessing. She had nursed him through his illness and he had said that, if she would have none of him, she had best go where her heart lay. So she sold up, took passage on the fastest clipper, and was waiting for me in a wee house in the city.

When it sank in I let out a whoop of joy that would alone have sent the Durack mob along the westward trail. I had no trouble in selling my claim and, gathering my few possessions, made haste to ship out to Fremantle.

The voyage was a gentle one for those rough northern

waters, so I could only attribute my queasy sensation to the fact that I was as nervous as a young girl. Imagine it, me, Sean Malloy, forty-one years old and the terror of the barmaids, no, - the darling of the barmaids from the Kimberley to Victoria, - shy? The fighter, the drinker, the teller of jokes and the weaver of songs was heading south to meet his bride-to-be as uneasy as a new schoolboy who has had an embarrassing accident! And somewhat uneasy in case my dream girl, who was now a mature woman of thirty-five, had budded, bloomed, blossomed, and was now nothing but a mean bit I'd be ashamed to pluck from the garden of womanhood.

We put into port at Carnarvon, where I was barbered. I bought a tidy suit and new small-clothes, a smart bowler and glossy boots. I had with me a ring fashioned from my own gold. by a Chinee man, who had also made an engagement ring from a small gem I had picked up on the great drive - a gem which gleamed green and blue and was shot through with a heart of fire. I had done what I could with what God had given me but my heart was like a cold bread pudding, or leaping, fluttering and changing by the minute as the coastal trader pulled alongside the quay.

I need not have worried. Clare was waiting, a slight girlish figure in sky-blue, golden wisps of hair escaping from a pert hat, trimmed with bluebird's wings. She came into my arms like a homing pigeon and I locked her to me closer than my heart. No words then. I looked, enraptured, at her sweet face, girl-soft from the Irish dew, and at the tiny lines age had written on her face. Her eyes were still so young, the same gaze which had been filled with tears when I left half a lifetime ago. All those years were as nothing and we laughed like children in our joy.

We were wed at once. I took a job in the city, the boredom and restrictions of it being lightened by the bliss of Clare's presence. But was it enough, I wondered, choking on the dirt and the sound of the city life? Oh, no! I longed for the bush. It had been my life, my way, for so long it had grown on me like a second skin. Yes, I longed for the bushman's way.

> *Rakehell bastard, drunkard sly,*
>
> *Care for nothing, red of eye,*
>
> *Trapped in the city at a desk 'til five,*
>
> *And I hate my life and I"m half alive,*
>
> *And I long for the bushman"s way.*
>
> *~*
>
> *A world of space is the bushman"s way,*
>
> *For the air is fresh and the air is free.*
>
> *There a man can search for his destiny,*
>
> *And I long for the bushman"s way.*
>
> *~*
>
> *Four walls prison me at home,*
>
> *Chained to a job, want to roam.*
>
> *Caught in the loving of my woman"s arms,*
>
> *And I hate the trap and I love her charms,*
>
> *And I long for the bushman"s way.*
>
> *~*

I read avidly of the new gold finds in the Pilbara. When Doyle brought in the Little Hero nugget, in 1885, I had marked it but was tied up round Halls Creek at the time. Now news was reported daily of not one but hundreds of nuggets from Pilbara Creek. Archie Clive wrote from Marble Bar to tell me of the area and when I read that he had brought in a veritable monster, the Bobby Dazzler, weighing 487 ounces, I was aflame with the gold fever again.

Clare watched with concern as the fires leapt in my eyes. I

would feel stifled by the four walls of our neat little dwelling and stride forth into the night to feel the cool air blowing and the rough bush or King's Park underfoot. Then I started drinking heavily and behaving in a generally disgusting manner.

Drown my sorrow, vent my spite,

Tell my tale to the birds of night.

Hating the pity and the selfish tears,

Months in town and it feels like years,

And I long for the bushman"s way.

~

Hate my job and hate the town,

Hate the traps that wear me down,

Like a bird I long to escape and fly,

With my love bird free in the open sky,

And I long for the bushman"s way.

~

"I've surrendered the lease of the house," Clare announced coolly over the breakfast table one morning as I sat, morosely nursing a large hangover. "Our passage north is booked for next week. I have written on this week's ship to Archie Clive, to assemble equipment for you. If you want any shopping done in the city before we leave, you had better tell me!"

I could only sit there, open-mouthed, muttering, "The diggings are no place for a woman."

Clare tossed her head and gave a small sniff of dismissal. I grinned as I recalled that Patrick had told me she was as obstinate as a mule. I realised that behind that fragile form there was an iron determination. It convinced me she could be one of the few to give life in the Outback a go.

She was practical, stoical and uncomplaining. By the time we had finished the sea voyage and the overland journey to the Bar, she had gained stature in my eyes. Not only was she pretty to fill the eye, loving to warm the soul but as tough as Irish oak. My God, I was proud of her. I felt she could come to love this strange country as much as I did.

The spinifex waves on the open range

Where the timeless hills are aloof and strange,

And the sunset floods the harsh red land with rose.

A land of promise; Soon men will follow and tame the wild.

~

There are pools of green under towering walls

Where the gorges echo with waterfalls

And the haunting sounds of unseen birds.

A land of promise; Soon men will follow and tame the wild.

~

There are rugged cliffs where the eagle flies

Through the shimmering air and the hot blue skies,

And where rests the drowsy old man kangaroo.

A land of promise; Soon men will follow and tame the wild.

~

For the dry earth waits for the first spring rain,

Then the bush is painted with gold again

And the mulla-mulla's distant purple hue.

A land of promise; Soon men will follow and tame the wild.

~

The water-hole mirrors the river gum

Where the air is filled with the insects' hum

And the blinding sunlight filters through the trees.
A land of promise; Soon men will follow and tame the wild.

~

The ghost gums cling to the dreamtime land
And the men who live here soon understand
That an empty land can fill an empty heart.
A land of promise; Soon men will follow and tame the wild.

~

In the 1880s, Marble Bar was the Queen of the Pilbara Goldfields, attended by Nullagine and Bamboo Creek, with Warrawoona, Peawah, Coongan, Mallina, Pilbara Creek and Cooglegong bustling around her skirts. They were all thriving townships in their hey-day but a thousand small claims and outposts lived and died unmarked. The town was throbbing with life. The wide streets were shaded by young gums in the heat of a relentless sun and all around was a brave new scene. Fine stone buildings were being erected or completed. The streets were filled with pack trains of mules or camels, horsemen from the stations, busy housewives, natty government officials, prospectors of every caste and creed and fancy ladies and their protectors.

Clare was thrilled. She exclaimed at every new sight, smiled happily at the small, dark children, and asked question after question. Archie Clive was waiting for us in the Ironclad, a smart new hotel, with wide verandahs where we took refreshment. He had obtained all the stores Clare and I had ordered, plus more, he indicated with a wink, knowing my inclination for grog. He also brought the proposition that we join him in the Carramine, a new claim he was developing where he had found good veins from surface specimens. We had worked together before and Clare had taken an instant fancy to the weather-beaten old rogue. She smiled and nodded her agreement.

We walked in the evening to the rocky bar of jasper across the Coogan River. We spent the night beneath nets on the beds on the hotel verandah. At dawn we left with Archie in his wagon.

The Carramine was a magic place. Spring water rippled from a small gorge into a pool. We built mulga and sacking homes beneath the shade of river gums. Archie and I mined ore and Clare started a garden. At night we sat down to delicious meals. Archie and I would fashion bush furniture while Clare mended and embroidered by the light of an oil lamp, around which huge moths fluttered.

We swam in the springs when the heat was vicious and often took mosquito nets at night to sleep in the cool air below the gum trees.

Everyone prospered. The digging was rich, the soil fertile and even Clare became plump. The Irish rose became a desert flower. Her warm golden tan was emphasised by her sun-bleached curls.

Weekly she would drive to Marble Bar with myself or Archie to get supplies and later she would go to the social gatherings with her friend Grace, who was the wife of the mining registrar. One trip she drove into camp at a furious pace and fell into my arms, laughing and crying all at once.

"You're to be a father, Sean Malloy," she cried.

I swept her off her feet and whirled her round with joy, yelling to Archie to break out the whisky for a celebration.

That night Clare was a queen. Archie and I had roasted a bush turkey. We cooked yams and fresh vegetables from her garden and feasted in the moonlight, We ordered her to bed early and then sat by the fire and drank and worried ourselves sick

"You'll take her to Perth before the wet?" said Archie.

I nodded.

"She's not young," I replied. "She must be near a doctor. We'll come back in April or May".

Next day we told her of the plans and she became a veritable termagant. She stamped and yelled and cried and then fell into a silence which lasted for days. She came to me one night as I sat by the creek, my head in my hands, lost in thought.

"Would you let me stay if I go to stay with Grace over Christmas and until the baby is born?" she whispered. "There is a doctor at the Bar and he is a good man. Oh, Sean, I love this place. I want to bear my child here, near to you and to the life we both love."

No one is more frightened than the mother from the country,

 Whose lonely days are full of fears for life that is unborn.

No one to share her worries and to fill her time with comfort,

 Imagining the darkest dreams, she prays she need not mourn.

 ~

No one is more lonely than the mother from the country,

 Who's had to leave her loved ones, her husband and her home,

 To travel to the city to bear a child in safety.

 She hears her new born baby cry and knows that she"s alone.

 ~

No one is more joyful than the mother from the country,

 Alone she studies face and form and tiny fingers curled,

 But caring isn't sharing, and happiness is doubled,

 When she bears her new born babe at home and shows it to

her world.

~

For caring isn't sharing and strangers' hands are colder,
Than ones who love and need you, than ones who really care,
For calmness isn't warmness and no words can console you,
Like loved ones silent holding as you bear your baby fair.

~

Oh, how could I say no. The gold country was my bride as well. Perth was alien to me, cold and empty. I swallowed sense, let sentiment prevail, and agreed.

A worse decision I could not have made.

The wet broke early, the week before Clare was due to stay with Grace. The road was cut. We waited for the rains to stop but they were relentless. I took the horse and tried to ride into town but the roads were impassable. As the days passed we grew more and more tense. Christmas was a day of false cheer and still the grey skies spread. We were limp from the humidity. Then the winds started. The dust rose and the bush grasses bent before the persistent gale. Archie turned grey and whispered, "Cyclone. God help us, Sean."

The cyclone is a big cat; the cyclone cat is wild,
Pitiless and merciless and wayward as a child.
Hot and heavy feral mists warn that the big cat prowls
And out to sea its temper grows with eerie, maddened howls.

~

Big cat stalks the waiting coast and tests its unleashed power
And, like a creature mesmerised, the landscape seems to cower.
Will the cat strike east or west and what will be its prey?

Big cat turns to smite the coast, then, teasing, turns away.

~

Big winds race from tropic seas and pounce upon the shores,
Tearing flesh from every hill with flashing, slashing claws.
Trees bend low before its might and snap like brittle bones.
The cyclone roars in anger and the tortured country groans.

~

Where the big cat cuts its path the rivers run like blood,
Death and wanton damage swept before the raging flood,
Leaving scars upon the earth. The old prospectors say,
Asked what force destroyed the land, "A wild cat passed this way!"

~

We raced the storm, moving our precious possessions to the mine shaft. Our mulga wood home disintegrated around us as the wind howled in frenzy. The horses were tethered near the creek. Archie raced down to bring them to higher ground. I heard his scream as a huge gum tree crashed across his back and the banks gave way. Archie's corpse was swept away in the raging red flood.

I led the horses into the gorge like a dead man, then went solemnly to Clare. She was bent over in agony. Her eyes were glazed with pain and she clung to me in despair. Dominic was born by lamplight in the eye of the storm, on the rough floor of the mine. The storm raged on. We nursed our fragile babe for warmth, in the silence of despair. Twelve hours later the storm died and with it our son.

Clare carried his tiny form from the mine. We gazed, hollow eyed, at the wreckage of our lives. The sky was a pale serene blue, and a watery sun shone from between the scudding clouds.

"Poor baby," she crooned to the tiny limp child. "You never

saw the sky or the sun. The world shall at least see you."

She cradled him in her arms and traced his perfect features with her fingers. We laid him to rest in a grave beneath the coolabahs and their leaves shed tears with us.

The mine was our home for days while we waited for the floods to subside. I was impatient to bring Clare to the doctor at Marble Bar for she was feverish and racked by painful cramps. The flesh melted from her bones and she became a shell. Hopelessly, I watched her fade, tormented in body and soul. My tenderest love was worthless when I held her gently as she shuddered in her final hours.

I buried her with the baby beneath the trees where we had spent our nights of love, and where our son had been conceived.

I rode away like a madman, wildly, aimlessly, through flooded claypan, creeks and gullies, through stands of acacia and eucalypt torn down by the fury of the gale. I came weeks later to the Bar, a starving, fevered wreck, and collapsed in the main street.

Grace nursed me back to health and sanity. I sat one evening weeks later, with Grace and her husband, on their porch overlooking the town. The damage had been horrendous, and I was not the only one who mourned.

"What will you do now, Sean?" Grace asked.

"I must go back to the Carramine," I replied. "It is not yet finished."

I had a stone to carve and an elegy to write. There, alone with my thoughts and my loved ones, I found the words and the strength to live.

I called my song Clare, for she was truly the music in my soul.

The diggings are silent. The miners have gone,

Far away, far away, far away. Who knows where?
But I cling to the silence where once the sun shone,
On my dear love, my true love, my own love, my Clare.

~

Now it's wicked for women whose menfolk seek gold,
Far away, far away, far away in the wild,
In the scorch of the summer or winter's sharp cold,
With my family, my dear wife and my only child.

~

Our shanty was sacking on mulga wood framed,
Far away, far away, far away, city lights,
But my Clare made it homely and never complained
Of the hardship, discomfort, the darkness and frights.

~

My little one faded away and Clare died,
Far away, far away, far away from all aid,
For my gold fever killed them. I sat and I cried.
For their pardon with sorrow for long I have paid.

~

Now the diggings are silent. I stay here alone,
Far away, far away, far away with my Clare,
And the gold that I glean gilds a roughly-hewn stone,
For my whole life, my dear wife and my child lie there.

~

All life needs is purpose, all fate left me was the mine. Now all I could give Clare was its gold, in penance. I stayed and plundered the Carramine and gilded that lonely grave with its riches.

The influenza is raging in me now. Its course is wicked in the tropics and the hospital at Marble Bar is filled with sick and dying men. Clare came to me last night and I know that I have little time to live.

We need no gold, my golden girl and I. Let the winds and the floods disperse it to the bush which reclaims all.

But, dear God, let my record remain, locked in this iron chest, that men may know that I have loved and lost and paid the price of chasing the golden rainbow.

Sean Patrick Malloy,

The Carramine, Marble Bar, 1897.

Tell It To The Marines

The great grey battleships were coming in to the port of Fremantle as Queenie reached the top of Monument Hill. From the war memorials she could see Rottnest Island, the hazy coastline towards Rockingham and Kwinana to the south, and the towering hotel at Scarborough in the north. The Indian Ocean stretched, blue-grey and white-horsed, as far as Africa. Queenie liked the feeling of space and limitless freedom the view presented. She did not like confined areas, the sense of being shut in, unable to do what one wanted, unable to go where one pleased.

"If I get reborn, I'd like to be a seagull," she muttered. "I'd like to wing across the waves and crap on the authorities."

She scrabbled in the depths of the old perambulator which was her constant companion to find a dog-eared copy of the Saturday edition of *The West Australian*. **US SHIPS HEAD FOR FREMANTLE** the headline announced.

'More than 4000 United States sailors and marines are due to arrive in Fremantle on Monday morning. The three day visit involves three ships from the US Navy's amphibious ready group that are returning to the US after a six-month tour of duty. The USS Peleliu, the USS Dubuque and the USS Comstock have been involved in operation Enduring Freedom, the global war on terrorism. They will not be open to the public.'

"Come on down, boys," said Queenie. "We're ready for you." She stuffed the newspaper back in the pram. Queenie was into recycling. Newspapers had good insulating properties. She'd need their warmth if she decided to sleep rough again that night. She'd found a nice position in the lee of the memorial, where the steps were wide enough to take her curled-up body and where the stonework on either side sheltered her from the sea breeze which had blown up during the early hours of Sunday evening.

She'd saved a sausage roll for breakfast and pulled out a half-full bottle of Coke to help it on its way. She was in no hurry. She knew from years of ship watching how long it would take the warships to come through the heads and tie up alongside Victoria Quay. She reckoned the sailors wouldn't be coming ashore until well after noon. By the time they started streaming across the bridge over the railway line which separated the docks from the town, she would be in position. There was plenty of time to spread her web and to wait, like a black widow, for a succulent morsel.

*

James Marvin Junior had downed a couple of cold beers in Clancy's Tavern but had no stomach for the pub-crawl his mates planned. He didn't like beer very much. Nor was he in the mood for what the wilder ones called rest and recreation. They might try to black out the thought of the savagery of Afghanistan from their minds, the scenes of butchery and destruction, the sheer terror of hunting the Taliban through the mountains. James Marvin Junior wanted to forget none of it. He'd already started writing it out, ready to slip into parts of the novel he was planning.

He didn't want to quench his thirst, despite the warmth of high summer in Fremantle. It beat the hell out of deep winter in Kabul, but all he wanted to do was drink up the atmosphere of the picturesque port, of old federation buildings, the stark prison high on the hill, and the quaint church in the centre of the town square. Turn your head to the right and see a cosmopolitan bustle of shoppers passing shop fronts unchanged for a hundred years, turn it left and see the modernistic shoe-boxes of the new civic building and the monstrosity of a concrete department store. But Kings Square itself was shaded by the wide-spreading boughs of ancient fig trees. He wanted a quiet place to think. There was a lawn area and a comfortable bench under a tree near the church porch.

He took the letter from his Army-issued jacket pocket and read it for the sixth time. He felt miserable. He made a mental note of how misery felt and shut his eyes. He drew in a deep breath, smelling the salt and the fish, the fumes of passing cars, the odour of bitumen softening in the sharp sunlight. Then he got a whiff of Queenie, who had sat down at the other end of the bench. She didn't smell bad, just different. Hers was the perfume of earth-covered potatoes, mingled with the sweet-sour of apples rotting in a barrel and a touch of something else which reminded him of rum. The old woman did not smell dirty or rancid, simply of old age and poverty. It was not like the sickly smell of starvation and disease that had marked the unseen women of Kabul, shrouded in their burkahs.

He glanced at the intruder into his comfort zone. The old woman was flopped across the bench like an unstrung puppet, her lined face relaxed and her eyes closed against the sunbeams which shimmered through the dappled shade. Her complexion was weather-beaten and the hair which straggled from under a crocheted cloche hat was white and rather oily. She wore the layered look, a singlet over a cotton dress over a dark shirt over a grubby lacy thing that peeped out at the neckline. She had well-worn black track pants under the dress. They were several sizes too small so the cuffs ended mid-calf, showing legs mottled with purple age spots and strung with over-worked muscles. Her socks were red and covered with little black mouse logos. The scuffed moccasins on her feet were coming unstitched and there was a hole in the sole of one.

"Had an eyeful, then?" said Queenie. "I seen you squintin' at me, like I was a specimen under a microphone. Din't your Ma tell you it was rude to stare?"

Marvin flushed. He felt embarrassed by the reprimand. "Beg pardon, ma'am. It's just that you remind me of my granny."

"Pig's bum!" said Queenie. "I bet your granny ain't a bag-lady."

"Why no, ma'am. She's a Presbyterian!"

"She a lady? Y'know, as in ladylike lady?"

"Yes, ma'am."

"I'm not. I'm a character. Tried bein' a lady. Din't like it. I ask you, could you see me drinkin' tea with me little finger crooked, doin' the pretty?"

Marvin grinned. "Can't say I can. You look like you belong in your own skin."

"You don't look like you belong in that camouflage gear. What you doin' in the Marines?"

"Seeing the world, ma'am. Fighting for democracy and the rights of mankind to live in freedom and peace."

"Cobblers! You just want to stick it up old Osama Bin Liner, wicked sod that he is. Shoot anyone?'

"Yes, ma'am."

"Me too. Din't it turn your guts?"

"I lost it, ma'am. Threw up my breakfast. Still get a ribbing from my mates about it."

"That why you're not with them?"

He wriggled uncomfortably. "Well, no. It's just that I got some bad news from Harper's Ferry. That's in West Virginia, ma'am. I needed to think about it."

He glanced across the square to the church, where there was considerable activity. Men and women, dressed in finery, were gathering at the porch. The men had flowers in the buttonholes of their suits, the women wore pretty corsages and wide-brimmed hats. The groomsmen were in dove-grey tails and the man of the moment looked green around the gills.

"That could have been me, next July," the Marine said.

Bright blue eyes looked at him calmly. "You want to talk? Get it off your chest? Like the confessional, talkin' to old Queenie."

James Marvin junior found, to his surprise, that he did want to talk to the old woman. She didn't repel him, she fascinated him. She called herself a character. Little did she know, but she might just end up as one, between the pages of a book. What was that about, 'Shoot anyone?' and the comment, 'Me too. Din't it turn your guts?' There was a story in this old biddy and he wanted it. He wanted it so badly he could almost taste the wanting.

"It's not the end of the world, Miss Queenie. May I call you that?"

"Queenie'll do. Beats all that ma'am stuff. Keep feelin' the Queen's standin' behind me. What's your handle, then?"

"James Marvin, ma'am."

"Marvellous Marvin. I knew a magician called that, when I was on the stage. Dancin' in a variety show. Proper trooper, I was. You look at these legs now." She stuck them out in front of her. "Wouldn't think they used to do the can-can, would you?"

The Marine was about to shake his head; then he let his mind morph, as he could do on the computer. He fed in the lines of Queenie's bones, rubbed off the wrinkles and rumples of old age and saw that, indeed, she might once have been a high-kicker. In fact, if one factored in the Scandinavian cheekbones and the blue eyes, removed two chins and the whiskers off her upper lip, she could have been a good-looking broad. Once.

"Call me Marvin, Queenie. I bet you had them drooling in the aisles. That's how I was about my girl, Peggy-Ann. Drooling. Making wedding plans."

"Engaged?"

"Nothing formal. Gave her my class ring. Talked about it, counting how many guests we'd ask and where we'd have the reception; how many kids we'd like. That sort of thing."

"You had a Dear John letter?"

"Not really. It's just she wants to go to college instead. Says we're too young and she wants a career before she settles down. Wants us to be friends, that's all."

Queenie's eyes narrowed as a limousine pulled up outside the church. The bridesmaids, in yellow tulle, emerged like petals from a rosebud.

"Very pretty," she said. "Very summery. Nice. Anyway, what's wrong with bein' friends?"

"I'm afraid I'll lose her. If Peggy-Ann goes to college, she'll meet other guys."

"If she loves you, it won't matter. Anyway, what's the alternative? If you try to hold on to her, to push the pace, you won't win. You're more likely to make her resent you. You tell her it's fine and you trust her. You tell her you're proud of her decision and say the more she grows and enriches her life, the more you'll love her."

"That's an act of faith, not of love."

"Hey, sometimes you have to let the things you love go free. I know."

The limousine with the bridal party arrived. "Hush, now," said Queenie. "I want a good look at the bride. Aw, ain't she a picture? All that lace and fine silk, beautiful. Brings a tear to the eye."

Marvin looked the petite girl, fair-haired and pretty, laughing up at her father, who was offering her his arm. The chauffeur passed her a bouquet of golden roses and she smiled her thanks.

Queenie, he was surprised to note, was quietly crying and trying to dab at her tears with a crumpled tissue. He passed her his large handkerchief.

"That's what I meant, when I said you have to let the things you love go free," Queenie said, wiping her eyes. "That bride is my daughter. Din't she look beautiful?"

"How can she be your daughter? I mean..."

"Go on, how does a dirty old bag-woman like me come to have a daughter like that? You think I'm a bloomin' liar, don't you? You really want to know?"

"I surely do."

"Her Pa was a Marine, like you. Came from Vermont, a big, fair-haired sergeant with eyes like chips of sapphire. Like you, down from the war on R and R, but his war was in Vietnam. We had a hell of a good time but he went back and was killed when your folk pulled out of Saigon. Never got to tell him I was in the family way. Never tried to get in touch with his family. Well, they'd got enough grief, hadn't they? I danced until I got too fat but the manager of the burlesque was a decent cove. He let me run the box office until my time came."

"Must have been hard."

"I was among friends, and that's not given to every woman, Marvin. There was nothin' for it, I was goin' to have the kid adopted. I knew I had to do it. How could I bring up a baby as a single mother, on the road mosta the time? So I went into this nursin' home. Very nice it was. Only two of us in a little ward and we were due at the same time. Nancy Armitage, she was. Married to a young architect. They were strugglin' but Alec was makin' a name for himself. She was fair desperate to start a family. I wished my baby could go to a family as warm and lovin' as those two.

"Anyway, we was delivered within hours of one another. My baby was a darlin'. My heart turned somersaults, I can tell you. Nancy's was a girl as well and, to look at them, the babies were much the same. But there was somethin' wrong with her delivery. They brought new-borns into the wards to be with their mothers in those days. It was ages before they brought Nancy back from the maternity ward and she was really groggy. They'd got her hooked up to a drip and all. And they din't bring the baby because she was too drugged to breast feed."

Marvin listened intently. Here was another tale for his collection of plots.

"I heard the midwife talkin' to the doctor when I was up havin' a pee," said Queenie. "Nancy's baby looked fine, but it wasn't goin' to live. They'd done a scan of the skull. Where there should have been a brain, there was just water. The spinal cord ended just above the neck. If the baby lived, it would be a vegetable. More likely the water inside the skull would swell and swell until it killed her."

"That's terrible."

"That's what I thought. Mind, I've since read in the Reader's Digest about some other kid born like that and the water went away in time and the brain blossomed out later, but I din't know that then. And I thought, there was little Nancy, about to have her heart broken, and there was my little darlin', about to go to God knows whom and me not knowin' if they'd love her or not. There's the doctor tellin' her to take her baby home and pray for a miracle, and her weepin' and still sedated, and her husband cuddlin' her and tellin' her he loved them both, whatever. And out in the Sister's office is the bitch from the Adoption Agency, ready to whisk my daughter away. So I did the sensible thing."

"Which was?"

"I took my nail scissors and some plasters from my bag...all dancers carry plasters...and swapped the babies' wrist bands. Nancy took my daughter home and her poor little mite went to the Agency. I heard it died a week later in Princess Margaret Hospital."

"And no one ever suspected?"

"Why should they? Nancy and Alec got a miracle and, because I knew who had her, I've been able to watch Kathy growin' up."

Marvin wished he hadn't given his handkerchief to the bag-lady. He had a strong desire to blow his nose. Emotion took him that way.

"We'll drink to her, shall we?" Queenie reached into the pram and pulled out two battered mugs. "I hope this is still cold," she said, pulling out a bottle of cheap champagne. "I had it in a cooler-bag but it's a hot day."

She ignored Marvin's protests about drinking in a public place in uniform and popped the cork. "Who's goin' to know?" she said. "Old tin mug like that. Could be water. Here, have a chicken sandwich. No, don't look like that. I didn't make them. Bought them from the supermarket this mornin', all sealed and kept cold as well."

It was a situation that was bizarre enough to appeal to

Marvin, who proposed a toast to the bride. The bubbles went up his nose and he spluttered. The sandwiches were moist and delicious. The picnic was a great success. It was a pity the shade of the tree had moved so they were in full sun but Queenie said they could find a new spot after the bride and groom came out of church.

When they did she thrust a packet of confetti into the Marine's hand and dragged him across to join those scattering rice and petals all over the newly-weds.

"That's Nancy," she hissed, pointing out an attractive woman in a deep pink suit. "You saw Alec. Handsome bugger, isn't he? Done really well. They own a big mansion in East Fremantle, overlookin' the river. Sent Kathy to the best schools. Lovely girl she turned out to be. Just lovely. Her husband's a star footballer. Comes from a good family. Old money."

The bridal party were shepherded into formal groups by the wedding photographer. He looked at Queenie with a scowl. "Oh, bugger off, Queenie. I don't want you in the background."

James Marvin junior, feeling the effects of sun and bubbly, suggested the man mind his manners or he'd flatten the photographer's lenses.

"Oh, piss off, Yank. Go screw a rag-head," said the camera man. "You want me to call one of your Redcaps to take you away for being drunk and disorderly?"

"There's no need for that, Bill Bryson," said Queenie. "You only had to ask nicely. We're goin' to sit in the shade." She flicked the brake lever and wheeled the pram under another Morton Bay fig tree. "This is my favourite place. I sleep here in summer, sometimes. I puts my pillow down between those two old big gnarly roots, wraps myself in a plastic tarpaulin, and I dreams like a baby."

"I like dreams," said Marvin. "What's your favourite? I mean, right now. If you had one wish, what would it be?"

"I wish I could've bought Kathy a weddin' present. I been dreamin' about for weeks, window shoppin', like. I saw just what I'd like to have given her. Waterford Crystal, it was, cut so it sparkled like diamonds, just the right shape for yellow roses like the ones she's carryin'. More than a hundred dollars it was, but so lovely."

James Marvin junior opened his wallet and peeled off a handful of notes. "You go and get it," he urged. "Get them to gift wrap it so that you can give it to one of the guests to give to Kathy. Just write, A Gift Of Love, on the tag."

"Thank you. It would mean a lot," Queenie said, quietly. "You'll stay here and mind my pram while I do the deed?"

"Sure thing, Queenie. The champagne's made me sleepy. I might nod off."

"Don't worry. No one will nick the old jalopy. You lean back against that trunk and think of Peggy-Ann."

*

The square was empty. It was the time between the closing of shops and offices and the serious business of enjoyment getting underway in the hotels and restaurants, at the sidewalk cafes along the Cappuccino Strip. The only life around was a flock of pigeons, pecking away at the rice grains among the drifts of confetti and petals outside the church.

An elderly policeman, on his way to the station for afternoon shift, spotted the young Marine under the tree. He noted the nearby pram and sniffed at the mug which had fallen from James Marvin's fingers. He shook the shoulder of the sleeper.

"Time to go back to your ship," he said. "You've twenty minutes to make it if you haven't got a late pass."

James Marvin shook his wits together and looked around. "Where's Queenie?"

"You been drinking with that old bag? I thought she'd be involved when I saw you with the pram. What yarn's she been spinning you?"

He listened to the Marine's account with raised eyebrows, trying to suppress the grin hovering around his lips.

"Your wits gone wandering, soldier? The Vietnam War ended in 1975. If Queenie had a baby by a Marine Sergeant from Vermont, the kid would be nearly thirty by now. That young woman who got hitched today was only eighteen. I know this because Sharon's father is my inspector. She got married mid-week because some damn fool of a bank-clerk has got her in the family way and it was the only day for six months they could book a reception centre. Secondly, Queenie's no bag-lady. She's got a perfectly good room and three meals a day in an old people's hostel. Did you give her money?"

"Yes, sir. A hundred and twenty dollars to buy a wedding present for her daughter."

"Well, she's down at the Fremantle Hotel right now, getting as drunk as a parrot. She'll not be back for the baby carriage. I'll just push it to the station and read her the riot act when she comes to collect it. She knows where it will be."

"Tell me, sir, was any of her story true? She said she'd shot a man."

"Well, if you hadn't believed the explanation I'd given you, I'd have told you that as a clincher. Queenie spent the whole of the Vietnam War years behind bars. She did ten years for armed robbery. She was a cold-blooded killer. She's done her time but she's as evil and as sly as a weasel. You don't want to press charges, do you?"

"No, sir. I'd rather not look a fool in front of my buddies."

"Good, because I hate paperwork. I didn't want arrest you for being drunk in charge of a perambulator."

"Thank you, sir. I'm going to be a writer but I haven't got Queenie's imagination. I reckon I've learned a lesson."

The sergeant grinned. "Too right, cobber. But if you're going to get suckered, get suckered by a good one. Queenie, without a doubt, spins the best yarns in Australia. She's what we call a spieler."

A gust of wind picked up leaves and confetti and petals and sent them twisting in an eddy across the square. James Marvin junior straightened his cap and squared his shoulders. He grinned. He could see the words of a story about the old bag lady forming in his mind as he marched himself back to the USS Peleliu.

It was a quiet night for the long arm of the law, which was aching. The police sergeant had spent most of the shift writing monthly reports. He was thinking about home, a beer and a plate of succulent ham sandwiches which the wife had promised to make up for him. He planned to enjoy a midnight movie before joining her in bed. In another fifteen minutes the night shift would come on duty ready for handover.

There was a commotion in the doorway and the sounds of loud, raucous singing. Rod Stewart's *Sailing,* came at him full blast and off key. Two young constables dragged Queenie into the station, trying to dodge her wildly kicking feet.

"Drunk and disorderly in the High Street," one panted.

The other found himself locked in Queenie's arms as she planted a kiss on his cheek. "Smashing, you are," she chortled. "Give us a dance, then!"

"Put her in a cell," the sergeant said, with a sigh. "She'll be less danger to herself than on the streets. You're a disgrace,

Queenie. Come on, turn out your pockets! Where's the money you rooked out of that nice young American?"

"Posted it to meself," she cackled, leering at him. "Think I'm daft enough to go on a lammer with two big ones in my pocket? There's some awful crooks in this town!"

"Fed that young man a right old load of rubbish, didn't you?"

"Him? Didn't you know James Marvin junior is my grandson? It was like this. I had an affair with his father when I was on tour with the Bluebells in Paris. Must've been in 1950, and him an engineer with the USAAF in Germany, down seein' how different Gay Paree was from Harper's Crossing, West Virginia." She cocked her head at the sergeant, like a cheeky sparrow, to see how he was taking it.

He wasn't. He was scowling awfully. "Queenie! Pack it in!"

She shrugged. "Oh, well. There'll be another mark along tomorrow! I'll tell it to the Marines!"

Hibiscus

There is a hibiscus flower behind my ear. My husband picked it and gently tucked it into my white hair, as if I were a young girl. I kiss two fingers and press them to his cheek. He is embarrassed by open displays of affection, although his eyes signal his love whenever they meet mine.

I feel a little foolish, for the young people beside the resort pool giggle as they watch us. I put my chin up and smile at them. They will have to get used to the habits of the geriatric guests for it is rarely a day goes by without me wearing a token of my darling's love. Today the flower has a golden calyx, flushing to deep pink. Yesterday's was crimson, its edges frilled and fluted.

"The hibiscus is a beautiful flower," he says, "And you are a beautiful woman."

Only he knows the significance of the hibiscus. It is part of my painful, shameful past. That past does not go away, but it is one which he accepts and, in so doing, the hurt is healed a little. One day I will be at peace with it.

I come from Broome, a tropical town on the northwest coast of Australia. My father, Mori Settsu, was a Japanese pearl diver. Two generations of his family had plundered the crystal-clear waters of the Kimberley for pearl oysters, seeking the shells which held spheres of beauty to please rich women. Barren oysters were not discarded. They are lined with nacre, mother-of-pearl which gleams with a soft iridescence like moonlight. They were used for buttons before man invented plastic. Each harvest was won at great risk. The diving suits were cumbersome. Huge, heavy headpieces, into which air was pumped, allowed limited movement on the bottom, and little protection against shark or sea snake. To come up too quickly meant nitrogen would fizz in the blood. The agony of the bends could kill or cripple. Many a lugger came back with a dying man. The cemetery was full of Japanese graves.

My mother could never explain her attraction to Mori, for he was a bandy-legged little man with a chest like a barrel, no catch for the blond Dutchwoman, who could have picked him up under one arm. Maybe it was the sweetness of his smile, or the deep purring laugh. Maybe it was because he treated her as if she were small, dainty and infinitely fragile, when she was, in reality, plain and stalwart. There was no doubt about their mutual respect and love.

I took after my father though with shapely legs. I was small and dark, with oriental features. My mother would look at me with wonder.

"Where did you come from, Mitsuko?" she'd say, smoothing my black glossy hair. "Your Papa looks like a monkey and I look like a horse, and you are a pretty little kitten."

"Papa says you found me under a mango tree," I'd reply.

"Ah, that would account for it. Strange things happen under mango trees."

I resemble Gertie round the eyes. Hers were a deep blue, Mori's dark brown. Mine are dark violet, wide and straighter than the almond slant of the Japanese.

Not that appearance matters in Broome, then or now. Many races live there in complete harmony, as friends. They built bungalows of corrugated iron along the dusty red streets, some on stilts to let the cool sea-breeze blow under the house. All had wide eaves for shade and storm-shutters to ward against the rage of cyclonic winds. All were surrounded by lush gardens, full of exotic plants. Exotic was normal in Broome. Intermarriage had produced children of many looks and colouring and I was just another variation. Little has changed.

I spoke Dutch with my mother, Japanese with my father and

Australian with my school friends. Languages came easily to me; I could talk to the Aborigines and had even picked up Javanese from traders who came to the import-export business for which Gertie was the secretary. Her family still lived on Java. We spent many happy holidays on their coffee plantation in the mountains.

I did well at school. My teachers predicted a bright future but Gertie said shorthand and typing were all I'd need and made sure I was competent in both. She hoped I'd join her in the trading post. I had other ideas. Most, I confess, were centred on my infatuation for Bill Paterson.

I'd known Bill since primary school. His father owned a cattle station to the east of the town and Bill was third in a large herd of brothers and sisters. They came in by truck every morning for classes but, at weekends, Bill and his older brothers would sometimes ride into Broome to watch the movies in the outdoor cinema. We were great friends. He went off to boarding school when he was eleven, but we stole time during the holidays to catch crabs among the muddy mangrove swamps, to fish from the rocks or swim off the sandy beaches. I rued the Javanese trips for they cut short my time with him, days which became increasingly more precious as we both reached school-leaving age.

"I'm going into wool-classing," Bill said. "I've got a place with a wool-broker in Fremantle. I'll only be back two weeks a year. Will you miss me, Mitsu?"

I looked at his slim, golden-brown body, the sun-bleached blond curls, the quiet grey eyes. He wasn't handsome, but he was very dear to me. I thought him wonderful for he could ride and shoot and bring down a steer with a rope.

"I'll not miss you that much," I said. "I'm starting as a probationer at Fremantle Hospital next month. I'm going nursing."

His eyes lit up. "Will you still be my best girl?"

"We can go to dances and to the movies. You know I'm your

girl, Bill."

"Only mine? For ever and ever?

It seems so simple looking back, but in such a childish way did we seal our future. It was not, of course, as easy as it sounded, for the matron ruled the nurses strictly. Our times together were limited. We learned to kiss and stroke and fondle one another but that was as far as it went. We dared no more, such were the standards of the day and so grave the risk of getting caught. Did we yearn for more intimacy? Perhaps, but in those days even the movies were very proper, very moralistic.

War changed everything. Bill enlisted and, as soon as I had my birthday, we got a special licence and married in secret. We dared not tell Matron. I had training to complete and married women were not allowed to nurse. Bill was in uniform but his duties allowed him enough free time for us to steal nights at hotels in Perth. Other nurses were in my position and we juggled rosters to help one another. If Matron guessed she turned a blind eye.

Those early months of 1940 were known as the phoney war. After the fall of France, Britain and Germany growled at one another but the horror had not begun. If the war was phoney, so was our marriage. What did I learn of love in this period? It was a fumbling, hesitant, embarrassed time of my life. It wasn't great. Bill wasn't a passionate lover. I didn't shrink from it. I was a nurse. Bill surprised me for, being brought up on the land, I felt he would be familiar with the principles of mating. While he knew the theory, he never seemed eager to linger over the act. It was, frankly, a period of disappointment, for I knew Mori and Gertie were enthusiastic lovers.

The week of Bill's embarkation leave was comparatively idyllic. A friend loaned us a cottage on the beach. For the first time we lived as a normal married couple. Bill read the paper as I cooked breakfast. He pegged out the washing so we could get down to the beach for a morning's fishing. He gutted the herring and cooked them on a barbecue. In the afternoons we dozed and made lazy love and at night we went to the pub. I plucked up courage to tell Bill the ways I might like to be loved and he lost his self-consciousness enough to make me a happy woman. By the end of the week I was pregnant and Bill was gone.

By four months I was showing and Matron gave me my marching orders. I took the coastal freighter to Broome as it was then the only practical way of getting there. My mother found work for me at the doctor's surgery and all seemed well until the sixth month, when I miscarried. I was heartbroken but the doctor pointed out the baby's backbone had not fused and it could not have lived.

"There'll be other babies for you and Bill," my father said.

"If I ever see Bill again."

I knew he was in North Africa. We'd worked out a code to avoid the censor's blue pencil on the few letters which got through. I knew the war in the desert was cruel. I was so depressed I gave up hope. Then we heard the Australians had taken Tobruk. I felt confident Bill would be sent home on leave. It was not to be. He was on the move, but only as far as Singapore, to combat the threat from Japanese troops who, having signed an alliance with the Axis powers of Italy and Germany, had invaded French Indo-China. By December the unthinkable had happened. The Japanese had declared war on the USA after Pearl Harbour and were sweeping through South East Asia.

Most distressing of all was when my father was arrested as an alien and interned. Gertie was bewildered.

"What do we do with our men gone from us?" she wailed. "Life is not worth living."

"Maybe I'll go to Singapore," I said. "Fortress Singapore is impregnable. I'll be safe there, and near Bill. I can work as a nurse again."

Gertie shuddered. "It's too dangerous. I'll come with you to Java and go to live with my mother and father."

Folly, all folly. Even as we were boarding the company's cargo boat for its regular journey from Darwin to Broome, Batavia and through the straits to Singapore, wiser families were trying to escape from the Dutch East Indies, as they were then known. We got as far as Java before we were strafed by a Zero fighter. Our ship, its steering damaged, ran aground near a small fishing village. While we were happy to have dry land under our feet, it was with almost disbelief that we saw Japanese troops approaching.

We were herded into trucks like cattle. There was no water, no food, no sanitation. There were old women and children. There were women traumatised by the death of loved ones and little girls crying for their fathers. We experienced three days of purgatory before we were told to get out of the transport and lined up behind the wire for tenko, our first formal encounter with the daily routine of roll call. We stood, like dirty scarecrows, in the heat of the sun. Only after two hours were we marched off to huts like those used for seasonal workers on the plantations. Older boys were segregated. The Dutch women were allocated huts on the lower slopes of the compound on a bare hillside. My mother and I were sent to those which had a mixed Australian and English component.

There was one thing all the women shared in common with the Japanese. They eyed me strangely.

"Chi-chi," hissed a Dutch wife, as she passed me.

"Eurasian slut," said a toffee-voiced Englishwoman.

"I'm Australian!" I gasped. My mother dug me in the ribs and whispered to be quiet.

The Japanese guards dragged me to the feet of the senior

officer. Was I Japanese, he asked. I looked blankly at him, pretending I did not understand his words. He laughed and told his sergeant I'd do for a start. He suggested the man pick nine more for his garden of flowers. Tomorrow.

They fed us watery rice with a few vegetables that night. We were so hungry it felt like a feast. It was a feast in comparison to the years of starvation which lay ahead. The sleeping platforms on which we lay, three of us to every four foot, under a thatched roof which let in the moonlight and a thousand biting insects, was luxury to limbs cramped for many hours in crowded trucks.

"They are picking young women," I told my mother. "You can guess why."

"It is always so, in times of war," she said. "There is no dishonour in surviving. I shall speak to the other hut leaders. They must only take the married women, those who know what a man expects of a woman."

"I have been chosen."

"I will not love you less. Do not let them know you understand what they say. You may learn much that's useful to us. Try to get quinine to ward against malaria. We will need medicines."

"Pray the Americans will drive these bastards back to the islands which spawned them," I said. "Pray this time will soon be over."

*

On February 15, 1942, Singapore surrendered. I knew my Bill was dead or himself a prisoner of Nippon. I hoped he was dead. That way he would never know what I had become or how I had been used.

I was Hibiscus. My room was between that of Lily and Cherry Blossom. Lotus and Chrysanthemum were across the corridor with Jasmine. Our quarters were those of the plantation servants. A dormitory had been converted into cubicles for Rose, Lavender, Paeony and Orchid, with a specially large room for fat, ugly Mama-san, who kept the bookings and imposed discipline. Mama-san also supervised the Javanese who cooked for us and the Japanese officers, who lived in the main house. She painted our flowers on the doors of the rooms because she could not pronounce our names and, indeed, we all wanted to forget who we were. We learned our Japanese titles and blanked out everything else.

The soldiers we serviced were camped on the old tennis courts or trucked in for recreation from outlying bases. I draw a veil over what those years were like. Lotus - the first Lotus - went mad. She screamed every time and tried to mutilate herself. She stopped eating and forgot to keep herself clean. She pulled her hair out and, in the end, was so unsavoury a sight Mama-san had her sent back to the work camp. She died soon afterwards of dysentery and malnutrition. The new Lotus was an English woman who fought every man who came near her. Some liked that. She paid for it in bruises and beatings but her eyes remained bright and her spirit undaunted.

I saw my mother sometimes as she trudged with the work gangs to the fields. I watched her getting thin and hollow-cheeked. I saw the great ulcers on her legs and the yellowness of jaundice on her skin. We smuggled food to the women's camp; sometimes extra rice or an egg. The Javanese helped us. I know my mother watched for me each day and would smile when she saw me. One day she did not come. I knew it was over for her. I cried for days. I was no comfort woman in the weeks ahead. There was no one to comfort me. It had been my one glimmer of hope, that mother and I would be reunited in freedom one day.

Mama-san shocked me from my lethargy. There had been a change of command. There was a new camp commandant and a new sergeant, one who was rumoured to be from the Kempetai, the dreaded Nippon military police. The sergeant, Kamato, was a brutal man, a sadistic man. I feared a return visit from him. Mama-san dismissed my protests. Unless I pulled myself together, she would send him to me every week, she threatened.

"I would rather die," I whispered.

"I expect you would," she snapped. "Hibiscus be a good girl for Mama-san, heh?"

None of us had good experiences with Kamato but it was the vulnerable who suffered most from his insatiable perversions. Lily had become pregnant despite Mama-san's insistence the soldiers wear condoms. An attempted abortion by our watchdog did not succeed, though Lily was so ill she was sent to the Dutch compound. The new Lily was only sixteen and terrified.

Kamato insisted he be assigned to her and, when Mama-san refused, beat the old dragon and tore up her appointment sheet. Lily's virginity was tight sealed and her legs hard crossed. The louder she yelled the more Kamato laughed. He took her like an animal instead. Her screams died away to sobs of distress. We dared not go to her; there were armed guards in the corridors, always. There was the sound of breaking glass from her room and then, an eerie silence.

We called on her to come to morning tenko but there was no reply. She was found hanging from the hook at the back of the door, the silken sash from her kimono round her neck. At her feet lay a broken mirror. Lily, battered and bruised, had not been pretty before her death. She was now terrible. Mama-san was very angry. She called the Commandant to look. Colonel Rikichi Kurita ordered Lily's body to be buried and the comfort house closed for the day.

The only flowers in season were hibiscus. We laid a posy of them on the grave.

Then we planned vengeance. The next time Kamato came

Cherry Blossom and I were waiting behind the curtain which screened a corner of Jasmine's cubicle. We were not on duty that night and the guards were distracted by a fuss Rose and Lavender created at the other end of the block. Cherry Blossom stunned Kamato with a blow to the head. We pulled him off Jasmine and rolled him onto the floor. I had the sash from Lily's kimono. I pushed one end down his throat and carried on feeding it into his gullet until the other end hung from his lips like a dark pink tongue. His face started to turn blue. It was my intention to pull out the choke when he was dead and leave no trace of what I had done. I knelt by his side, my fingers holding the end of the silk, waiting. The door was flung open. The Commandant stood there, his face impassive. He took my place beside Kamato, then pulled out the sash. He slapped the sergeant's face until he inhaled again. Colour returned to his cheeks.

Colonel Kurita stood in front of me and took my face between his hands. "I could not let you do this, little Hibiscus," he said. "Your heart would have died inside you."

I spoke in Japanese without thinking. "My heart has been dead for many years. My heart died when your people brought me to this place."

"But you are Hibiscus. The flowers die quickly and new blossoms open. The hibiscus is a symbol of eternal womanhood."

"What your men do here does not destroy the flowers of my heart, but withers my being at the roots. My very essence is brittle and the sap runs dry in my spirit."

His eyebrows were raised. "What are you doing here? You look like a daughter of Nippon, you speak like a daughter of the Empire. You think like a geisha."

"I am Australian," I said. "I will defy the Rising Sun until it sets!"

He bowed. "Ah, so," he said.

The guards took Kamato away. We only saw him once again.

The next day was a full roll call. The Commandant ordered Kamato to be dragged into the middle of the parade ground. He spoke to the sergeant sternly and ordered me to translate.

"Colonel Kurita has reminded the men the comfort women are there for comfort, not for abuse," I said. "He has told Kamato he is a dishonourable dog. Had he been a man of honour he would have ordered him to fall upon his own sword, but he says Kamato is not fit to die like a man."

The Commandant nodded as I fell silent and stepped back into line. Then he drew his revolver and shot Kamato between the eyes.

Life was easier afterwards. There was no more roughness, no violence. I was singled out by Kurita for his favours. Every seventh day I would be marched down to his rooms. We did the tea ceremony, we talked. That was all. He was an educated man, a cultured man. His English was flawless, accented but correct. He talked about his wife and daughters, who lived in Tokyo. He talked about his family in Nagasaki. He grew quieter as the tide of war swung against the Nippon Empire and as the American bombers started pounding the Land of the Rising Sun.

We made love only once, the night he learned his wife and children had died in the fire-bombing of the capital. Then I gave him comfort and, in compassion, found passion which had been lacking in my love life, even in the days with Bill.

I went to him once of my own accord, when news of the bombing of Nagasaki reached us. The camp was in confusion as the talk of surrender spread. I ran in fear, and took the sword from his hands.

"No. You shall not do this, Rikichi," I said. "It makes no sense. You are a man of intelligence and humanity. Your sort will be needed to rebuild your country. A man of honour will work for the future, not die for dead traditions. Rikichi, the peace will be as hard for your people as the war!"

He took my hands and kissed my fingers. "I shall always remember you, little Hibiscus," he said. "May sunshine come again to your heart. It is deep and darkest night in mine."

*

After peace there was a bitter season. Bill came home, a pitiful figure, even after weeks of rehabilitation. I was ready to love him to bits, but our union was quick and unsatisfying. He cried afterwards and told me he did not want to sleep with me again.

"I hate the Japanese, and you remind me," he whispered. He flinched if I so much as touched him and his eyes could not meet mine.

I moved into the spare room of the cottage we were renting. It was a relief for me, too, for if truth be told, I never wanted to entertain a man again although I carried a seed in my womb. I knew malnourishment would explain much. I had more urgent things to think of, such as the job the Patersons found for me, secretarial work with the Pastoralists and Graziers, in the city. Bill was sick and his pension did not even meet the cost of the spirits he had turned to for comfort.

It was a wicked winter. Bill came home one night drenched and blue with cold. He was shivering and yet burning hot. The influenza turned to pneumonia and, within a week, he was gone. Sick though I was, I brought his ashes back to Broome.

Frank Paterson, his eldest brother, who now ran the cattle station, met me off the ship and ran me home to my father's house. Father was pathetically glad to see me. He had aged dreadfully in the internment camp and was lost without Gertie. He bustled about making tea while I talked to Frank.

"I found these when I was going through Bill's effects," I

said, handing him a slim bundle of dog-eared letters and a faded photograph. It was inscribed, 'To my darling, your ever-loving Roy.' The snapshot was of a fair young man with a slim moustache above full lips and a gentle chin.

"Did you read the letters?" asked Frank, skimming through them.

"Yes. They explain a lot about Bill which I did not understand. No hard feelings, though, Frank. I'm glad he found love in that hell-hole."

His brother sighed. "Bill was always like that, even at boarding school. We were surprised when he married you, but pleased. We thought he'd outgrown it at last."

"Oh, he could play the man," I said, sardonically.

"So I see." Frank patted my swollen stomach. "So I see. Are you staying in Broome?"

"No. I've a job to return to. The company's promised me work at home and I've rented a house with another war widow, in much the same position."

"You could come and live on the station. The Patersons look after their own."

"You just keep an eye on my father, Frank. I'll look after the baby."

I wrote to the Patersons three months after Michael was born. I told them the baby, though premature, was healthy and a good weight but that, sadly for their sakes, he did not look like Bill, but favoured the Settsu blood. Maybe I should have been ashamed at the falsehood but I had learned that survival has its own code of honour.

*

I rarely went back to Broome, especially after my father died. His mind went and he knew no one in his latter years. Frank found him a place in a nursing home and assured me of his comfort. The Patersons were true to their word and continued their support, sending me money each week and paying for Michael to go to Guildford Grammar School when he was old enough to board.

Ironically, I could probably have afforded the school fees myself by then, for I was working as a highly-paid interpreter for the government. Japan's economy was booming and it was a time when the Japanese were eager for investment in Australian resources. I escorted delegations and hosted functions. I sat in on business meetings and negotiated deals which would ensure the future of Australian interests.

I recall the reception at Parliament House, when the tall, white-haired Premier beckoned to me. "Mitsuko, I'd like you to meet the new envoy from Hyogo Prefecture. Mr Rikichi Kurita tells me you are old friends."

He bowed and kissed my hand. "We share an interest in gardening, Mrs Paterson, do we not?"

I blushed. The diplomat took my arm and asked me to show him around the grounds of the Parliament. The Premier nodded dismissal.

We walked and we talked. Oh, how we talked. We were, indeed, old friends. Rikichi stopped underneath the first hibiscus tree we passed and picked a pink bloom of Apple Blossom. He tucked it behind my ear and then, shyly, he kissed me.

"I have wanted to do that for twelve years," he said. "I thought I was in an eternal winter when my family died and our country was brought to its knees. But I never forgot you, Hibiscus, nor your words. Your memory kept the sap running in my veins."

"I had a more tangible reminder of you," I said. "Your son is very like you."

Oh, the wonder on his face! The sheer joy which lit his eyes!

The smile which slowly spread and the arms which enfolded me tightly.

"You have given me the Spring, Mitsuko," he cried.

The Japanese are a dignified people. Rikichi, as Michael's grandchildren would say these days, lost it. He took my hands and danced me across the lawns until, in a quiet recess under the wisterias, he was able to kiss me with all the passion I deserved.

*

Rikichi Kurita has never stopped dancing me through life. For more than forty years he has loved me and our son, with a quiet intensity which has made all our days a summer of happiness. And every day he places a hibiscus behind my ear and tells me how beautiful I am.

Now, while we can still manage it, he has brought me home at last to Broome. We have visited my father's grave and that of Bill, and put flowers beneath the plaque in the church which is my memorial to my mother.

So we walk, hand in hand, through the Japanese-inspired resort hotel and down the path to Cable Beach, to watch the full moon and its reflection on the ocean. It is very beautiful. Scores of other tourists watch with us in silence. I have a basket on one arm. It is filled with flowers which the hotel gardener said we might pick.

Rikichi and I take off our shoes and paddle in the gentle waves on the sand. I take the hibiscus from my hair and set it to float on the moonlit water. Then we kneel, stiffly, painfully, to send the red and orange hibiscus blossoms from the basket drifting down the ladder of light. It is incredibly lovely, this rite of passage. I feel cleansed and so, I know, does Rikichi, for he shares the shame of what was done to me. Soon the spirits of Rikichi and I will float away like that, purified, gently into the eternal light which waits behind the darkness.

We say nothing. We do not need to speak. He kisses my hand again. That says it all.

The Hole Truth

I burnt down Loxington School. I pleaded guilty then and, even though I was just a lad, I paid the price. I stood in the dock in the stinking-hot court house on Loxington Green and scuffed my feet. The magistrate frowned at me. The court was packed with angry people. They didn't have a single good thought about me, I could tell.

Can't blame them, I suppose. They'd worked long and hard to raise money to build the school, with the help of a stingy government grant. They'd held raffle drives and whist nights and community dances. The cockies had donated sheep for spit-roasts and barbecues. The local timber mill had given loads of karri planks and the parents and their parents before them had spent days in the harsh Australian sun, sawing and hammering and painting.

They had made sure there was somewhere decent to educate their children. They'd dipped into their savings to pay for a piano for the big hall, in memory of the boys who went to war and never returned. They said it was better than a memorial and their sons had fought for the future of the Loxington children, not for bitter memories to be graven in stone.

There'd been a town party when classes moved from the old buildings, soon to be the kindergarten, and I was as happy as any kid around. I could understand the community's feeling. The piano went up in flames along with the rest of the school. Books, blackboards, records and sports equipment were utterly destroyed on that fateful night. I pleaded guilty because I caused the fire. Not that I meant to. I was only after one desk, one darn desk - that's all.

I had many hours to think about events during the time I

spent in a reform school, for that's where I ended up. I offered no defence then and I can't think even now that I could have done any differently, because who'd have believed me? I never told anyone why I'd done it; not my Mum and Dad, not the police, not the magistrate, not even the priest. I figured God knew and reckoned I'd done the right thing.

That desk. That one darn desk. Here I sit on the verandah, rolling a smoke, and looking out across the paddocks, wondering why the heck I've drifted back to Loxington in my old age, when I've spent most of my life battling round the world. There's a lot more understanding about scientific things these days, but I still can't explain what happened that summer.

I was in my last year at the board school. I was maybe twelve, thirteen years old, itching to get out of class and into a job. The school might have been new, but we couldn't afford to throw out the old furniture. The parents carted over the chairs and desks from the ramshackle hut we once used and scrounged round for extras from auction sales and the like. The big hall was a barn of a place, with a high roof, spanned by open rafters where birds crept in to roost. They dropped cack on the floor overnight.

There were three groups in there, all looked after by one teacher, Mrs Hatcher, a sour-faced old biddy with a soul like a crab-apple. She spent most of her time with the younger kids. She'd given up hope for most of us. Most of my peers were as fed up with book-learning as I was, so we had a fair whack of idle time on our hands.

My desk must have been made a hundred years ago. That's what it looked like. It was solid wood, with a lid that lifted with a squeak and a hole at the back for an inkwell. The inkwell was made of china with a little dipper hole into which we had to pour dark blue sludge that stank like old dishcloths. We had no biros, no felt-tipped markers, just pens with loose nibs which were crossed and scratchy. Ink ran all over our fingers. We were always blotting our work. I liked blotting paper; it mushed up just as if I'd been chewing pith.

I knew my desk was old because there were names and initials carved in it. One was done by my uncle and another, my mate Harry said, was the name of his grandfather. So it just went to show. There were a couple of cracks and knots in the wood, and a hole someone had made with a compass point.

That's what started the trouble. That hole. When old Hatcher wasn't looking I used to soak paper in the inkwell and pack it into the hole, pretending I was the school dentist. You'd never believe how much it would take. And the next day it would have dried out and I could give it another go. Sometimes I'd pinch a bit of chalk and mash it up with spit and press that in. Other times I'd chew up the crusts from my lunch or stick an apple core or a bit of cheese rind into the cavity. I never wondered where it was all going. It wasn't inside the desk and it wasn't outside the desk. Maybe the birds pecked it out at night, or a mouse had eaten it. That's what I thought.

The desk in front was where Joan Crosby sat. She was the bank manager's girl and one of those smartypants who get right up your nose. She had freckles and glasses. The whine in her voice was like the sound chalk makes when it squeaks on a blackboard. It made your ears crackle. She was teacher's pet and, what's worse, a sneak. She was a tell-tale with a big streak of mean. Her only good thing was her hair. It was the rich red you get on a kelpie pup and was shiny as a new penny. She wore it in a plait so long she could sit on it.

I stayed away from her and her meanness as much as I could, but she fair dropped me in it the day after Mum made up a batch of treacle toffee. It was that sticky, chewy sort. Mum had tucked a couple of chunks, wrapped in waxed paper, inside my dinner box. The thought of it was too much. I'd popped one square in my pocket and I'd rubbed a finger on it and licked it off a couple of times. My stomach was fair crying out for the sweetness. I knew the rules. If I was caught it would mean a caning, but you know how it is. When old Hatcher stopped marking books and started writing problems on the blackboard, I was out with the taffy and into a good chewing session.

I was six chomps on the way to Paradise when Joan piped up, "Mrs Hatcher, somebody is eating sweets." She turned and looked right at me and smirked. Mrs Hatcher came stomping down the row and ordered me to spit it out. Well, I couldn't. I'd already palmed it and was trying my darnedest to push it into the hole in the desk.

"Open your mouth," she yelled.

I showed her my tonsils.

"Lift your hand!"

So I did. But there was nothing there. I had to empty my pockets and turn out my desk and that was a right performance. All the time I was wondering where the toffee'd gone. The hole was empty. It was as if the desk had eaten it, I thought, remembering the way it had seemed to suck and tug on my palm, like a greedy mouth. That was an interesting idea but not one to dally over because I was on my way to the principal's office to get six of the best. Old sour-face reckoned I must have swallowed the toffee. But on my way out of the classroom I quietly lifted sneaky Joan's plait and slipped the end of it in the hole.

The principal whipped the cane back and fore in front of my eyes, making it whistle eagerly. I held out my hand for the cuts but it was already bleeding. There was a raw patch, as if a great blister had burst. So he whacked my bum instead. It stung like blazes but I had no time to dwell on it. I could hear the commotion in the big hall as I crossed the yard and I ran there as fast as misery would allow me.

Joan Crosby was arched back over my desk, screaming blue murder. Hatcher was yelling for help and the little kids were crying. Joan's head was flat against the desktop and her hair seemed to be coming out at the roots. Her eyes were popping out and she yelled for help when she saw me. How she thought I could solve the problem I didn't know, but I pulled out my penknife and started sawing at the plait. In the middle of her scalp her skin had been sucked deep into the hole which seemed to be pulsing like two angry jaws. I expected her to bleed when I cut, and she did. But then there was a funny sort of plop and some of the skin and goo went into the hole and the scalp sort of puckered and sealed, leaving a raw bald spot the size of a pigeon's egg, just like the mark on my palm. She looked a right mess, hair all shaggy and chopped and a sort of dazed look in her eyes.

I got the blame, of course. No one mentioned the fact that I'd been out of the room getting a walloping when the panic started. I didn't argue too much. I felt guilty at having messed with her hair. Nobody gave two thoughts about what had caused the trouble; mass hysteria they'd call it these days. They assumed I'd attacked Joan for having tittle-tattled.

Nobody even asked where her hair had gone, let alone what had caused the blister on her head. And was I going to try to explain? Make me laugh, will you? Look, back when I was a lad we didn't have things like science; we had a healthy fear of the unexplained, of magic and hauntings and things that went bump in the night, but we didn't understand things any better than most people today. I just reckoned I'd taught an unknown something about hunger, and it was getting greedy. But no one was going to call me daft if I kept my mouth shut. So I did.

When my mother and father were called to the school and told I was expelled, I didn't protest. Dad got me an apprenticeship with a carpenter in the next town, Ashburton, twelve miles away. I lived with Fred Turbey and his missus in their attic. I was so tired after a day fixing and fencing that work, food and sleep were all I thought about, except for a game of cricket at the weekend.

I was so busy and interested in my new life that I didn't think much of the Loxington drama until young Jack Kent went missing. Jack was a no-hoper. He was a runty kid to start with and, as well as getting up at daybreak to do the farmyard chores his lazy, drunken lout of a father avoided, he got little more to eat than pig swill. There was a bad fever going about and Jack came out in a muck sweat in the morning. Mrs Hatcher had told him to have a sleep on the desk during the dinner hour and told Joan Crosby to stay with him until he dropped off. Joan was no longer a smartypants. More often than not she was as vague as a moon child. She went off to play as soon as Jack was driving home the pigs. When the bell rang for classes to start Jack was nowhere to be seen.

They never found him. They hunted the bush for miles around; they dragged the waterholes; they crawled into mine shafts and looked round fresh-turned ground in case there was a grave. Most reckoned he'd simply run away from home, and no one blamed him. It was days later that I found out that he was now the one who'd sat behind Joan Crosby, at my old desk. I tell you, I'd not have put my head near that hole. I reckoned that a beast had fed.

That was why I cycled to Loxington with a can of petrol. I only meant to burn the desk. I soaked it with petrol and left a stub of candle burning under it while I made my escape. I was tucked up under the Turbey's roof and fast asleep before the desk caught fire and the blaze spread to the entire building. Those that raised the alarm and saw the school burn said it sounded as if a great giant was threshing around inside, spreading flame from roof to walls, groaning and screaming. The heat was so fierce no one could get near until the walls themselves were consumed by the flame.

And do you know what they found in the morning? Nothing. Not a timber, not a brick, not a smouldering beam nor a metal bar, not even the iron framework from the piano, and that took a lot of swallowing. It was as if the school had never been.

They arrested me. Joan Crosby had seen me cycling past with the fuel can. She was, of course, still a sneak. I could not put up a good defence. Who'd have believed me? Her evidence would have convicted a saint. The funny thing was that, when the police marched me past the scene of the fire on my way to court, there was a rumbling sound from the earth like an empty stomach during a Sunday church service.

They never rebuilt the school. Every time they brought a load of bricks on site, they vanished. Nearby homes started to lean and crumble. The shire engineer reckoned there was subsidence from underground caverns, like those at salt mines in Cheshire, in Britain, into which whole houses disappeared.

Loxington people found they couldn't keep dogs or cats any time at all and kangaroos and bandicoots were no longer seen in the bush. In time anything metallic left lying around, like rakes or spades or even wheelbarrows, seemed to be drawn towards the school site. They left skid marks in the dirt. The ground shook.

Parents began to send their children to school in Ashburton where there was a new State Housing Commission estate. As soon as their names came to the top of the public housing list, they moved. Loxington was a like a ghost town in a few years and, when the pub closed, even the die-hards chose to die easy in the new aged persons' homes in Lower Ashburton.

The shire put a fence round the edge of Loxington. The electricity was cut off, the Water Corporation dug up the mains and the Roads Board put No Through Road signs on all approaches. It was less than ten years before the Government took the name off the maps.

So why did I come back? I'd made a pretty good living at my trade. I had money in the bank and was a lot wiser in the ways of the world. I'd done a lot of reading and a lot of thinking over the years. I reckoned I knew what was what. So I'd done a deal with the council and a couple of the metropolitan local authorities. I built a depot, hired a bulldozer and went into business. Every day trucks rumble into base and tip out the stinking garbage of the cities. And every night I start up the dozer and push the rubbish towards the hole.

It's grown bigger and greedier. The cavity I teased into a maw is now a great slavering pit, eagerly gobbling as much food as I can give it. I don't know where the garbage goes. I don't even care.

I handle it warily. I never drive too close. I'm going to make sure that hole doesn't get me!

That's nothing but the truth!

Backyard Bliss

Madge Gingell smiled for the television camera. "Len Prentice has been so kind to us," she said, flapping her eyelashes at Hamish Jury, host of the new gardening makeover show, The Lawn Rangers.

"Do tell us why your neighbour deserves his garden restyled by Channel XX," the talking spade suggested, sticking the microphone under her nose and beaming encouragement at the plump young mother, whose fashion sense was eighteen and rap when her figure was thirty and matronly.

"It was very hard for little Jimmy and I when my husband lost his job at the bank and could no longer support us. Should I say the bit about him going down for seven years for embezzlement?"

"Cut!" snapped Jury, running his fingers through the trademark mop of blonde curls. "Let's take the intro again, Mrs Gingell, and no, don't mention your husband's whereabouts. Just explain about the pride he took in his garden and how hard you've worked to keep it the way he liked it, after he'd gone. The viewers will assume he's dead. Then talk about Jimmy's illness and how Mr Prentice helped you by paying for the flight to America so the surgeons could operate on the tumour on the lad's back."

"Yes, I see." It took six takes before she got it off pat, concluding with, "and I don't know how he found the money, because he's only got the pension."

Jury glanced at the adjacent homes. Neither was top of the range but Mrs Gingell's was spick and span. It looked as if she polished the bricks. Len Prentice's walls were rust-stained, the mortar crumbling, paint peeling off the gutters, putty loose around the window panes, several of which were cracked.

"Get some wide-angle shots to show the difference in the gardens," he told the crew. "Now, you're sure the old boy will be away for the weekend?"

"He always is. Regular as clockwork. He leaves on Friday morning and comes back on Monday night. Never says where he goes. I reckon he stays with family to save having to cook a Sunday roast. 'Had a nice time?' I asks him. 'Good as gold,' he says. Doesn't talk to me much. Chats away to our Jimmy. Lets Jimmy and his friends kick a football round his yard. Says they can't break anything because he hasn't got much interest in gardening. Does a bit of digging on a Monday night; that's his lot."

Hamish looked at the barren block which had a few straggling rose bushes next to the fence, a weedy top growth where there should have been lawn, and a few concrete slabs around the Hills Hoist washing line. The surface was uneven, unkempt, though there were patches of disturbed sand where the old man had obviously been digging and had planted a small bed of radishes, a couple of tomato plants, an isolated row of sweetcorn, gone to seed.

"You say the Police and Citizens' Boys Club are coming to give his house a lick of paint on Saturday? They'll keep out of our way?"

"Yes. They'll do the back first and concentrate on the sides and front while your gang does the remake of the back garden. They're happy to cooperate. Mr Prentice donated them a trampoline last winter and paid for the boys to go to the circus."

"Mrs Gingell, you do understand that you and Jimmy must stay out of the way while we work? We don't want you on camera again until the welcoming party. You've done your bit."

She tittered. "If there's anything else you need, pop over. Toodle-oo!"

*

There was quite a buzz up and down Croker Avenue after the Lawn Rangers were seen in the area, having shot the opening sequence. The neighbours knew all about the makeover but no one let on to Mr Prentice. The old boy left as usual on Friday morning and, no sooner had he driven off in his battered old four-wheel-drive than the sticky-beaks turned out in force to watch the television stars arrive.

Whacko Bates, the intrepid and comical rustic carpenter came first, directing the behind the scene workers to unload great stacks of fence panels finished in a mock stonework design. Bessie Baker, known to viewers as Boobs, changed from city clothes into the overalls she wore on top of very little else. She enlisted the help of the painters to carry in a small forest of shrubs in plastic pots. Julian Martin, the heavy-duty bricklayer, directed the bobcat to level the garden. And all the time the camera crews recorded the action.

"We're not going to change the levels," Jury explained to the viewers. "The owner is elderly and we feel that steps or terraces might be difficult for him to handle. As you can see, very little has been done since the house was built, the only attempt at decorative treatment being the black vertical lines Mr Prentice has painted on the fences, a foot apart. Well, those will go, concealed behind the mock limestone panels we'll clad the boundaries with."

The cameras cut to the design the Lawn Rangers had developed.

"I'm bringing in more limestone blocks to edge deep beds at the end of the garden where the owner can grow vegetables," said Julian. "As you've seen, he enjoys planting seeds but the sand here gives no nourishment to them, so we will backfill the beds with a good mix of compost, worm castings and topsoil. As they will be raised, it will save the gentleman having to bend to cultivate his crops."

Whacko, already busy on construction of a pergola and deck outside the back door, wiped his brow, leaving a streak of green paint which an enthusiastic club member had splattered in his hair.

"We'll put green canvas sails as awnings," he said. "This will match the new paintwork and contrast well with the weathered limewash we'll apply to the decking. In front of this will be a paved area in thick sandstone, which Julian is going to secure in a base of gravel and cement. That will stop them moving. Mr Prentice will never have to worry about weeds again."

Boobs smiled toothily and lisped. "No, because I will mulch around the globulosa furnicota and the ataxian spirulis longifer with which I'm going to fill the interesting flower borders that Hamish is digging to mask the sides of the garden. When he moves on to his major task, I will begin planting a mass of these ornamental grasses and ever-hardy trees. What exciting plans have you got to individualise this garden, Hamish?" she cooed.

"As you can see, I'm struggling with this coil of plastic hose," he said, leering down her cleavage. "It will go under the decking, under the sandstone slabs, and will emerge in a pre-cast mock-rock koi pool with a fountain. I can imagine the old gentleman getting hours of enjoyment from sitting on the edge, watching the fish."

Oh, what fun they all had, sweating in the midday sun, being drenched by an evening thunderstorm, digging, delving and playing tricks for the cameras. By Monday afternoon all that remained to be done was to sweep up the dirt and hose down the sandstone. Hamish Jury turned on the tap to test the fountain in the koi pond.

Young Jimmy was called in to film his sequence, his own

special on camera thank you to his benefactor. As directed, he slid the bag of goldfish into the water and watched the large gold, orange and white koi make themselves at home among newly planted waterweeds.

"You oughtn't to do that," Jimmy said seriously. "My schoolteacher says you should let water settle for three days before you put fish in an aquarium. He says the chlorine will kill them. I bet they'll kark it."

"Cut!" snapped Jury. "Cut that last bit. You silly boy, we can always buy more. We have to do this now, for the programme."

Jimmy sniffed. "Well, I don't think Mr Prentice will like this. I don't think my Mum should have brought you here. I think he liked his garden just the way it was."

Hamish Jury's stomach lurched as if a large toad were doing gymnastics in his gut. He had a feeling of impending disaster. He could feel a public relations nightmare coming on. His grin felt as if it was plastered on but he kept the facade in one piece until the old man drove into the carport and joined Mrs Gingell, Jimmy and the Police and Citizens Boys' Club for the celebrations. The look of surprise on the face of Mr Prentice was very dramatic.

"And no more weeds blowing over the fence," said an enthusiastic Mrs Gingell. "Oh, isn't it beautiful!"

"A garden is a lovesome thing, God wot," quoth Hamish, wrapping up the show. "That's it, folks. Another programme in the bag."

"That's as maybe," Mr Prentice growled. "Now you can take your fancy bricks and sticks and stones and effing goldfish back where they came from. And I mean now, before I call the police and have you charged with being illegally on my curtilage."

Hamish winced. "You don't mean it?"

"I do. Let alone the damage to my property, there's the wee

matter of trespass. Oh, a fine law suit it will make."

"Can't we talk this over?" Hamish cried. "Come to some settlement?"

"Maybe, but we'll talk it over in the kitchen, you and I. I'm not wanting the world to hear what I have to say."

The inside of the house was neat as a pin. Mr Prentice took a bottle of Scotch from a cupboard and poured two heavy drams. He waved Jury to a seat at the kitchen table and unrolled a chart which he took from the drawer where others kept knives. The chart was squared off and was a mass of faint numbers.

"Now, young man. How much dirt did you dig from my garden and where did you dump it?" he said.

"We haven't taken any sand out; we just moved it around a bit."

"That's one blessing. You'd have had a hell of a job on your hands bringing it back otherwise. You see the chart? You saw the black lines on my fences? Each of those fence markings is a line on this plan, Mr Jury. I'm a prospector and I hate paying taxes on what I find. Every Monday night I come back from the bush and I dig a hole and bury a couple of nuggets, maybe more. It's not often I come home empty handed. Then, when I want to buy something or give my friends a helping hand, I get out this chart, work out how many ounces are in which square, and dig them out again. And you, you dumb lubbock, have turned my garden upside down."

"Oh hell!" Hamish was white. "Compensation, you said. How much?"

"Lad, there's close on half a million dollars in my back yard, buried under your handiwork. Do you think your network would cough up that much? You know what you're going to do, don't you?"

Hamish Jury nodded.

"Mind, I'll still want some compensation. Shall we say $100,000? It will take me a year to dig it all over and find what was there. But this time I'll put it in the bank, I reckon. And this, I insist, is between you and me. I don't want your crew pocketing my nuggets."

"Agreed," said the Lawn Ranger, shaking the old man's hand. "I'll refuse to explain what this is all about. When shall we start?"

"Oh, now would be fine." Mr Prentice took the whisky bottle and carried it outside the backdoor, where he settled back in the rustic armchair on the new limewash decking. He might, he thought, let them leave this part of the design intact. He might even get them to move the koi pond to the Gingell garden, because young Jimmy would like that.

He sat and sipped while the Lawn Rangers, astonished and cursing, started prising up the flagstones, taking crowbars to the underlying cement, shovelling out potting mix and heaving up sandstone blocks. Whacko stripped the panels from the fence, swearing as he hammered his thumb. The crew members were seething with anger and tired as old dogs. It was gone midnight before Len took pity and allowed them to go home.

"You'll be back at first light?" he suggested. "I'd like my garden back as soon as possible."

It was quiet in the wrecked garden after the Channel XX team had gone. Mr Prentice stretched and yawned. It was past his bedtime. He heard the quiet grate of fibro as a loose section of the fence was pushed aside. Young Jimmy, playing hookey.

"Your mother will tan your bum if she finds you out at this time of night," he said gently. "Go on. Get yourself an orange fizzer from the kitchen."

Jimmy popped the tag and sneezed as the bubbles went up

his nose. "Well, Uncle Len, did it work?" he asked.

"Swallowed the yarn hook, line and sinker. I'm glad you told me what your mother was planning. That was a good scheme we cooked up."

"It was wicked fun painting the lines on the fence."

"Wicked, yes. Fun, maybe."

"There isn't any gold in the garden, is there? Not really?"

Len Prentice, who'd spent two weeks replacing the bricks in the cistern with small jars of fragments and had hidden big specimens in the plate-warming drawer under the oven, tapped the side of his nose. "Mine to know, yours to find out," he chuckled.

Jimmy grinned and touched his can of fizz to the old man's whisky glass. "Cheers," he said. "It's great. Now we can still play footie in your yard and cricket in the summer."

"You can indeed. Now, off to bed, you scallywag!"

Jimmy gave his friend a hug and squeezed back through the fence. Len Prentice poured the last of the Scotch into his glass and watched the moon go down.

"Ah, bliss!" he sighed in contentment, looking at his ruined back garden. Mind, he was a little concerned about Jimmy, who showed every sign of having as devious a mind as his father. Look where that had landed Gingell senior. In the slammer!

Len smiled. In another couple of years he'd start taking Jimmy out bush with him, teaching him the ways of the outback, the honour and sense of responsibility of the true blue Aussies.

"Why, lad, you'll discover the whole of Australia is your backyard," he said.

The Boy

Miss Spindleberry had no business getting pregnant at her age, the busybodies said. What was worse, she refused to name the father, thus denying the opportunity to confirm widespread speculation that it was the well-muscled scion of an old and respectable family.

What Gerald lacked between his ears, he compensated for with what was between his legs, they said. He had propositioned every woman in Barking Creek and laid a good few of them, especially when the men were off shearing or on fencing contracts at distant stations. Gerald was always in fine fettle during the football season, when the supporters' club packed fans into their battered old bus and followed the local team to away matches. Gerald never left the Tablelands. Nor did Miss Spindleberry.

Of course, no one dared ask her the question direct. The librarian was never forthcoming about her personal life. Deafness afflicted her when she was asked for her first name. She appeared to have no family in the area yet had moved into Longmuir House without a dollar changing hands. The bank manager believed her to be a long lost cousin of the late Claude Longmuir and said she had inherited it quite legally after a lengthy court-room battle with Claude's estranged wife. As no one in Barking Creek had liked Mrs Longmuir, who had run off with another toff from Melbourne, they were content with their new neighbour, even if she was quiet. Even if she was weird. Even if she was a Green. And rather hippy.

Her greatest idiosyncrasy was a fondness for the Appalachian harp, which she played while singing, in a high, sweet voice, folk songs from Turkey and the Lebanon. She'd sit on stage, slim as a willow wand, her dead straight hair loosened to fall in a pale waterfall around her ethnic blouse and home-spun shirt, and place her clumsy instrument on her bony knees. She'd touch the hammer-keys and pluck notes from the many strings with a tortoiseshell pick. She'd been invited to entertain at concerts in the town for three years. Then no one had asked her again.

Instead she went to folk festivals. There was a school of thought that the baby's father was one of the alternative people who had camped at Lake Tinaroo for the Rites of Spring. There had been a low mist over the caravan park for a week afterwards and some said it smelt of strange and illicit substances. Miss Spindleberry had been seen there with a tall, thin man with white hair in a pony-tail. When Mrs Marker, from the shop, asked who her friend was, the librarian had said, "Just that. An old friend. He makes dream-catchers."

"It just goes to show," Mrs Marker told the Country Women's Association meeting. "She's not the maiden lady we all thought. We all know what goes on with those hippy types and the weirdos from Nimbin."

"Dream-catchers are the work of the Evil One." Jennifer Kingsbury was paranoid about religion. She'd shot her dog when it had peed against the cross on the War Memorial. She'd spent the next three days on her knees, with a bucket of bleach, trying to wash out the mark of blasphemy.

Miss Spindleberry merely smiled a tight little smile with her tightly pursed mouth and resigned from her position at the library. The postmistress said that money was telegraphed to her every week so, whoever the father was, he was obviously prepared to support her. That reduced the odds on it being Gerald who could have slipped a tenner under her front door, or down the front of her bra, if he were in truth an intimate of hers.

"You'd never get a tenner down her bra," said Mrs Marker. "She's got no more than two half hamburger buns up top."

Brenda Jones, who doubled her duties as district nurse with

those of midwife, admitted her nose was out of joint. Miss Spindleberry had booked an alternative birth-mistress from Cairns and wanted her attendance purely as an observer and to meet the requirements of state law. She bit her bottom lip and corrected Mrs Marker. "That's not right," she said. "She's filled out in the last month. She's a 38D if she's an inch."

There were many curious eyes in Barking Creek, just as there are in any small country town where boredom beats television for entertainment. Outback Australia is like that. There's so much of nothing going on that small changes take on an otherwise incongruous importance. Miss Spindleberry grew in unexpected ways. She carried the bulge low and deep, sticking out her bum to accommodate the swelling rather than letting it ride proud of the hips as other women do. And, because she pushed out her chest to maintain balance, the melons were very prominent.

The baby was born in an inflatable plastic swimming pool in the lounge room. The birth-mistress and Miss Spindleberry inhaled herbal mix from an ornate hookah. It was an easy birth for a first timer. Nurse Brenda, who was asked to hold crystals over the water at the critical time, reported that the child was seven pounds in the old measure and a very long, thin baby. Its head was elongated, not the round, featureless pudding of most new-borns. It had a face with a heavy jaw and a high, bulging forehead. It looked, in fact, rather like Miss Spindleberry.

"She's called it Boy, though if you ask me, there's a bit of doubt about that," said Nurse Brenda. "It's got ever such a little willy. It can't be Gerald's. I think it might be a cross gender baby, you know."

"A spermanthrocite?" Jennifer Kingsbury was agog.

"At least we won't have to lock up our daughters in ten years time if it's one of those," Mrs Marker sighed. "I couldn't have born to watch my granddaughters go through what we had to put up with when Gerald was on the randy."

Miss Spindleberry seemed happy enough with the baby. She pushed it down to the shops in a very ornate old-fashioned perambulator she'd found in an attic at Longmuir House. The women examined the new arrival critically. It was a very pale-skinned infant, with long, bony hands that waved around like the tendrils on a sea anemone. The ends of its fingers were wide and spatulate, like the pads of a tree-frog. The school children, who were reading The Hobbit, having been taken to see Lord of the Rings at Atherton, immediately nick-named him Gollum. Boy did not hiss or whisper, nor did he cry as others did. His was an unnerving howl like a Siamese cat on heat. As he grew older he did not say, "Mamma," or, "Dadda," but merely went, "Ungh ungh," in his throat.

The one thing Boy did do well was grow. He fed well, said Miss Spindleberry to Nurse Brenda, who had a professional interest in the child.

She watched Boy fondly as she put him to breast. He drank greedily, sucking hard from the very start, seeming to pull nourishment right from her very toes. Her nipples were stretched to long udders, hard and sore with the drag on them. She rubbed lanolin into them and packed her cups with cotton wool in a bid to keep them dry, but they dripped terribly. It was easier to let Boy suckle than keep herself clean so she spent most of the time feeding him. At least he did not come to her hungry, for then he would bite and gnash on her flesh in his eagerness.

If anything, her milk supply increased and the need to wean Boy never seemed to occur to her. Even when he cut his first teeth she persevered. It was agony when those sharp blades bit into her flesh but, though she often whimpered, he was allowed to drink his fill. Boy seemed to like the taste of blood. She tried to put him onto the bottle, expressing herself delicately with a hand pump, but he bit through the rubber teat and howled like a banshee.

"Rub bitter aloes on your nipples and put honey on the teat of the bottle," suggested Nurse Brenda, who doubled as infant health adviser. "You can't let him go on chewing you up. Look at the state you're in. Don't you realise blood is seeping through the front of your blouse?"

She was concerned for the mother, not the child. Boy was the size of a year-old baby by the time he was six-months old. He was very strong and very wilful by eight months. He bit when he was given injections. He glared angrily when nurse tried to open his mouth to check the alignment of his teeth. He fastened onto her finger and clung on like a pit-bull terrier. Miss Spindleberry had to hold his nose and cut off his breath before he would let go. Brenda Jones swore she would never look inside the little monster's mouth again.

Boy punished his mother that evening. She cried at supper time. She dressed her wounds with anaesthetic cream and put cold compresses under her arms, for her lymph nodes were swollen with infection. She tried to feed him cereal but he spat it out. She tried lambs dinner and tinned apple, prunes and custard and beef broth. She refused to let him suckle for days, fearing the bacteria in her system would poison her milk. Her breasts became so engorged that it was simpler to let him draw off the excess. Miss Spindleberry drank half a bottle of gin before she let him near her. She fell asleep with Boy on the bed with her. When one dairy ran dry, he crawled into position on the other and polished that off too.

This became a routine. On waking she would do the washing and slip back into bed to feed Boy. She would lie, exhausted, until past midday while he crawled around the house, doing whatever he wanted to do. He'd be back on the teat for lunch and would sleep, locked on like a joey in the pouch, for an hour or so. His mother would pry him loose and leave him snoring and whiffling while she folded the laundry, made herself a sandwich, fed the cat, and phoned through a grocery order to the shop. She no longer had the strength to walk down the main street. Mrs Marker delivered.

"No!" she screamed at Boy. "Cover your teeth! If you bite me again I'll not feed you."

He snarled at her and drew blood. She clipped him a ringing slap around the ear. He spat and hissed.

"I mean it," she threatened.

Boy capitulated. He sucked in his lips and tugged at the milk bar without laying dental enamel to flesh. "Good boy, Boy," said his mother. "I knew you could understand me. You're not stupid, are you?"

Despite his lack of vocalisation, his mother, who had spent the last months of pregnancy reading about early childhood education, was convinced of his outstanding intelligence. As with many alternatives, she firmly held that the first three years of life were those in which a baby was most receptive to instruction. What started with object recognition cards progressed to simple reading books. She would point to a word and Boy would put his finger on the right symbol or point to matching objects around the room. "Ungh, ungh," he'd say, and nod at her. As soon as he had enough control of his movements to turn a page, she started leaving books in his playpen. He never tore them or scribbled crayon on the pages. He seemed to read them and, when he came to the last page, would grunt until she exchanged them. She was not daft enough to claim the baby could read. She had no desire to be laughed at and, after all, who was she to tell? She had never made friends in Barking and did not find motherhood drew her into a wider circle of acquaintances.

How could she join the mothers' club when there was so little time between feeding Boy one meal and the next? She knew they would be shocked to learn he was still suckling and not on cereal and orange juice and good stuff that came in baby jars or had been pushed through a mouli. Boy's appetite remained voracious.

The toddler said, "Ungh, ungh," in between great gulps. Lunch didn't taste as good without the flavour from the biting, but he'd discovered that hard sucking drew nutrient from the fine capillaries around the nipple. He left Miss Spindleberry's side and looked back at she who fed him. It had been getting harder to get a good flow. The milk bags were withering. When he had finished they lay flat on her ribs, flabby pouches of skin. She was not mothering him properly, he decided. He found the cat food. The minced beef had the right sort of taste.

He had been walking for weeks. He was getting the hang of self-sufficiency. He could reach the handle on the refrigerator door and could tug it open. He knew what he wanted. He was a child of the television age. He had seen advertisements for milk. Boy sat on the floor and drank the remainder of a carton. He saw the newly-opened KITFIT and ate it with his fingers. Then he turned on the TV and selected the right channel for Playschool.

*

It was a year later when Nurse Brenda became alarmed by the deterioration in Miss Spindleberry's health. Her menstrual cycle had not returned after Boy's birth and she showed all the signs of a rapid transition to the menopause. "It's as if that child has sucked the very life out of her," she said to Jennifer Kingsbury. "And just look at the size of him. He's like a five-year-old and strong! You wouldn't believe how strong he is."

"But not talking," said Mrs Kingsbury. "Is he, you know, all there? Or is he going to grow up one of those big simpletons like Loony Pete from Upsandowns?"

"Hard to say," was the reply. "I'm driving Miss Spindleberry and Boy to the district hospital next week. She's found a lump in her breast and, when the specialist has looked at that, I'll whip Boy into the paediatrician for his annual check."

Miss Spindleberry insisted on sitting in the back seat so she could feed Boy. Brenda Jones was sick of the sound of slurp and suck by the time they reached the big town. Boy was eager to be set down and followed his mother down the corridor to the mammography unit. He got so agitated at the instruction to, "be a good boy while Mummy has her picture taken," that Nurse Brenda had to take him into the room and stand behind the protective lead screen, holding him, while the mother laid her poor, worn out dugs on the little platform under which the X-ray plates were inserted. Boy yelled in protest when the technician brought down the top part of the mammography machine and compressed the milk factories. He yelled, "Ungh, ungh, ungh," and made sucking sounds. The technician, noting the blood staining the milk that was smeared on the platform, shook his head at Brenda. She knew without a doubt what would appear on the plates.

"It's widespread in the breast tissue and has invaded the lymph nodes," said the specialist. "It means a radical mastectomy of both breasts and follow-up chemotherapy and radiology, Miss Spindleberry. How far it has extended we don't yet know but we'll postpone further tests until after the operation. For now, I'll take some blood to run routine tests."

Boy watched the doctor stick the needle in his mother's arm with great interest. "Ungh, ungh," he crowed as the blood flowed into little vials.

The specialist laughed. "Didn't you know that your Mummy is full of red stuff?" he chuckled. "Here, in these blue lines. You've got them on your arms, too. That's where she keeps her good stuff!"

"Ungh," said Boy, in satisfaction. It explained a lot. There were blue lines in the milk factory.

The paediatrician was very interested in the grunting child. Miss Spindleberry, still in shock at the news of her own condition, obeyed the young doctor's orders as if in a dream. She tried to lift Boy onto the examination table but he was so heavy Nurse Brenda had to help her.

"I want to look inside his mouth," the doctor said. "Have you noticed any abnormalities, nurse?"

Brenda Jones shook her head. "He bites. I've never been able to get past his teeth."

"Well, you won't play that trick on me," said the doctor, sticking a sedative injection in Boy's arm. "There, now he's relaxed, let's have a look. Hold his body, mother, while nurse opens his jaws for me. Ah, as I thought. He's tongue-tied. Look, mother. His tongue should be loose and flexible but it's fixed to the bottom of his mouth by soft tissue. I'll just freeze it and then cut it free with a cauterising scalpel. This will seal off the bleeders as we go. There. That's done. And we'll whip the foreskin off his little willy while we're at it. We'll keep him in the children's ward for a few days to make sure he doesn't swallow his tongue. He'll only want to eat ice cream and jelly, I expect, but then he can go home."

"I won't be there," Miss Spindleberry said bleakly. "I'll be in here, still."

"You are not to worry yourself," Nurse Brenda stated firmly. "It won't hurt him to be fostered for a few weeks. Mrs Kingsbury is very good like that. She regards fostering as part of her Christian duty."

"You will make sure Boy gets lots of milk. And meat. He likes meat."

"Never fear. After all, isn't Jennifer Kingsbury married to the Barking butcher? Boy will feel quite at home."

Boy showed no interest in his mother after he came round in a cot in the children's ward. He was too sick to eat but drank a cup of milk before lights out. His mother had, he felt, subjected him to such indignities that any sense of affection he had held for her was irrevocably gone. He was hopeful when they brought him red jelly the next day but spat it out in disgust when he discovered it was sweet and smelt of strawberries. He consented to eat ice-cream but threw up blancmange, custard and rice pudding. He bit the arm of the personal care assistant who was feeding him.

"He drew blood!" the woman protested. Boy licked his lips appreciatively. He got no further chance to bite though he tried. He was handled with care by attendants who wore long rubber gloves when they had to change his willy-wadding or wash his bottom.

Six days later he was taken back to Barking by Brenda Jones. Jennifer Kingsbury was by no means sure she wanted Boy, but felt very sorry for his mother who had, after all, done her no wrong even if she had never done her any good. The woman was, however, a good customer of the butcher, who appreciated the size of the Spindleberry weekly order of pet meat.

"I don't know how many cats she feeds, Jennifer, but they eat well," Ted Kingsbury said. "Liver, minced steak, diced kidney. She doesn't buy much for herself, except the occasional chop or a ready-to-roast chicken."

"You're a fine one to talk. You give Lassie the same sort of diet. Wasteful, it is, what that dog is fed."

"Lassie needs nourishment," her husband said. "She's got ten pups to feed, after all."

Boy liked the Kingsbury house. It was full of good smells,

being adjacent to the butcher's shop. He drank two cups of milk, having mastered the art in the hospital. He eyed the bowl of dog meat and decided he'd have that when the bitch wasn't looking.

Mrs Kingsbury tried to get him to say,"Thank you," instead of,"Ungh." The nurse had told her there was now nothing to stop him talking and Jennifer was determined to have him chatting away before his mother came home. "Please may I leave the table?" she said. "Come on, try to say it."

Boy glared. "Ungh," had done so far and he saw no reason to deviate from a word that had covered all possible responses in the past.

"Don't upset him," said Mr Kingsbury. "It's all strange to him, remember. Come on, lad. I know what you'd like. You'd like to play with the puppies."

Boy did like. The bitch didn't. She backed away into the corner of the outhouse where the butcher plucked chickens and skinned rabbits. Boy crawled towards the dog, ignoring her whining, grunting as he fixed his eyes remorselessly on hers. She bared her teeth and whined. Boy bared his teeth and growled. He grabbed her long, floppy ears and spat on her nostrils. She slavered in submission.

"Making friends, are you?" said Ted Kingsbury, coming out with his knives, which were ready for their nightly sharpening. He laughed as Boy leaned back against the bitch's side, heedless of her shivering flanks. The puppies scrambled over the child, rolling about and making him laugh with their antics. Boy was surprised to find he could laugh. He watched the puppies panting with excitement and found he could stick his tongue out and do that too.

"Now, lad. Let old Lassie feed the pups in peace. You come with me and I'll show you my rabbits."

Boy had already noted that Lassie had an interesting milk factory. He planned to exploit it later. He followed the butcher down the garden to the rabbit pens. He was allowed to hold one and stroke its ears while Mr Kingsbury cleaned out the hutch and gave it fresh water and food. There were twenty hutches, many holding six or more furry animals, so it took some time. When all was done, the butcher took a list from his pocket and consulted it. "Three for the hotel," he said. "Right." He reached into a pen and dragged out wriggling rabbits. He broke their necks with a quick jerk. Buy gave a grunt of surprise. "You want to watch me skin them?"

Boy nodded. He sat at the butcher's side and watched the dead things being hung on hooks and the deft skill with which the paws were severed and the skin pulled off in one piece. A sharp knife cut into the stomach cavity and the entrails were pulled out into a bucket. "That muck'll go to the tallow works," Ted said, dropping the head on top of the guts. "But not these bits. These are the best bits of the lot." The butcher held out a huge palm, on which rested a rabbit heart, kidneys and liver. "Not a lot, but it tastes good." He cut off a sliver and popped it in his mouth.

"Ungh," said Boy.

The butcher laughed. "Want some, do you? Here, try this!"

Boy chomped eagerly. It was good. He laughed and pointed to his mouth again. "Ungh, ungh, ungh."

"You want more, you ask properly."

Boy nodded. "Please."

"Right. But don't you tell my wife what you've been eating. She likes her meat baked to a cinder. I'm a rare man, myself."

The bond was formed. Boy spent most of his time with the man of the house and as little as possible with Jennifer Kingsbury. She tried to take him to church but he howled his strange caterwaul throughout the early part of the service. The preacher suggested his foster mother take him to the creche in the parish hall where Sunday School was in progress. Boy, who had never before come into close contact with other children, bit a little girl who tried to give him a lollipop.

"Why, you nasty little monster," said the teacher. "Sit in the corner!"

There were books in the corner so Boy was not dismayed. There was little to read at the Kingsbury's, except butchery manuals, the CWA cookery book, a thick tome on family health and another on Commercial Rabbit Production. Other than those, Jennifer's taste ran to slim romances on the covers of which impossibly handsome men embraced beautiful women with big milk factories. Boy whisked through seven chapters of Stories from the Bible before he was rescued by a flustered mother-figure.

"You mind him next Sunday, Ted! I'm not taking him to church again, if he's going to misbehave and make a fuss. Biting like that. You should have seen that poor child's arm. Worse than being mauled by a Rottweiler, Doctor Badgery said."

"What, was old Badgery in church? You mean they let the poor old sod out of the nursing home? He's well past his use-by date, I can tell you. Senile dementia, his sister told me."

"He's not so senile that he can't worship the Lord. He has his good days, they tell me."

"Must be getting ready to pull up his roots then, for you'd never get Badgery in a church when he was younger. In the pub, yes. He used to say he should have been a lawyer for he was always getting called to the bar! Aw, well, then. Looks like you and I'll have to watch footie instead, Boy."

Getting on the coach with the big butcher was fun, Boy

thought. They rattled along the roads through farming communities and ended up in distant towns on playing fields where men would run and kick and jump for the oval ball. Boy got used to eating sandwiches, made with thick slabs of rare beef which turned the bread soggy and pink. There was always a bottle of milk for him in the cooler in which Ted Kingsbury kept his beer. If Boy felt really desperate, he would wander off in the second half of the game and find a snack. He had spotted a pocket knife in the shed and kept it very sharp. There was often a sleeping cat to be found or, if such prey was not available, a cow or sheep might be mesmerised sufficiently to allow him to open a vein and take a quick drink. He left people alone. They talked.

His mother came home after three months. She was weak and depressed. Mrs Kingsbury visited and asked if Boy could come home. Miss Spindleberry shook her head. "Please keep him for another day or so," she asked. "After that, I'm going off to recuperate. He can come with me."

The tall, thin man with the long white pony-tail drove into town in a van painted all the colours of the rainbow. Miss Spindleberry was waiting with suitcases packed and her Appalachian harp under her arm. Boy sat by the side of the road, sulking. Ted Kingsbury had brought him over and was now chatting to his mother about this and that. Mainly that, but as the woman had no interest in football, he got little reaction.

Boy did not like the commune. He did not like alternative music. He did not like the smell of the whacky baccy or the vegetarian food. He did not understand when his mother agreed to take powders that made her forget her pain and play around until she fell into an exhausted sleep. Nor did he like the man with the pony-tail who told Miss Spindleberry she was still beautiful even if she had no breasts. They all went naked in the moonlight. Pony-Tail looked at Boy's little willy and laughed. Miss Spindleberry laughed too and said Boy did not take after his father. When Pony-Tail got off her and went back to play games in the caravan he shared with two teenage girls, she fell asleep. Boy looked at her bare chest in disdain. He crept towards her mattress and took out his knife. It only took a tiny snick to open a vein in her arm. He fed.

There was plenty of interesting reading material in the commune, about medicine and spirituality and comparative religion. There were herbal recipes and spells for good and bad fortune. He found texts on white and black arts. There were lots of big words and olde worlde writing in some of the heaviest volumes. Boy conned them all and, at last, knew what he was. It made him smile to have a sense of identity, to know that he was not different, that there were others like him.

Miss Spindleberry got sicker and asked to be taken home. Boy sighed with relief. Her blood was thin and unsatisfying. She was driven to the district hospital and admitted for a few days to have a transfusion. Brenda Jones had begged the Kingsburys to take him in again temporarily. After that, she said, he might have to go into permanent care, to be made a ward of the state, for his mother was clearly unable to look after him.

Ted was happy about the arrangement but Jennifer was not. After Boy had left earlier there was always meat left in Lassie's bowl. She realised with disgust that the child had been stealing food. She refused to allow him to accompany her husband to the football. There had been gossip about strange goings-on. The CWA network was active in the country towns near Barking Creek.

Boy's reappearance coincided with the Master Butcher's Convention in Brisbane. Jennifer ordered her husband to lock the shop and put Lassie in kennels. The pups had already found new homes. She shut Boy in the bedroom and slept in an armchair in the kitchen.

Boy was hungry. He climbed out of the window and made his way down the garden to the rabbit pens. His knife was very sharp. He didn't try to skin the furries. He just slit the bellies and pulled out the good bits. The sixth rabbit screamed, as those in the wild do when confronted by a weasel.

Mrs Kingsbury woke up and checked the child's door. It was still locked. Nevertheless, she took a torch and the poker, nervously determined to see what had made the noise. She found the child with his face in the guts of his next course, surrounded by carcasses. She screamed and hurled abuse at him.

"What are you doing? What are you?"

"Ungh, hungry," he said, licking his lips.

"I'm taking you home, right now. I don't care if your mother has just come out of hospital. She can put up with you, for not another hour are you spending under my roof. You're not natural. I don't know what you are, but you're not natural."

Boy knew what he was and told her. He told her at great length while she dragged him down the road to Longmuir House. He told her what she was, as well. Having found his voice, he told her very loudly. He had to do so to drown out her hysterical screaming.

Lights had come up all down the main road by the time Mrs Kingsbury staggered back to her own home. Neighbours made her tea and listened as she cried and embroidered and was violently sick in the sink. The men fetched spades and buried the animal remains.

Boy, who had been locked in the room with his mother, smiled at the woman who was staring at him, wide-eyed. There was a mess of medicines on the bedside table and a tray of congealed food.

"What have you done?" she whispered. Boy told her. She sat

up, painfully, shifting herself hard back against the bedhead. "Keep away from me." There was panic in her voice. She grabbed at a knife left on the Meals on Wheels dinner.

"You've eaten," Boy said accusingly. "I'm hungry." He giggled to himself. The knife looked very blunt. He stealthily opened the blade in his pocket.

He knew what had to be done. He knew what had to be said. He'd seen it enacted on television many times. "Mommee, I love you Mommee!"

Miss Spindleberry's face crumpled. She threw the knife away and opened her arms to Boy. He had never called her Mommee before. He had never said he loved her. She held him close to her heart, showering his head with kisses.

"Mommee, gimme your heart!" Boy grinned and plunged the knife into her chest.

Nurse Brenda was furious when she heard what had happened. "You locked that little monster in with his mother? Are you all mad? God knows what he'll do."

She turned her back on the astounded throng and pushed her way out of the Kingsbury kitchen. There was silence at Longmuir House. She, who was nervous when out at night, took the mace spray from her handbag and readied it.

She unlocked the door of the bedroom and threw it open. The scene was much as she had feared. Boy lay on the bed, his mouth full of something dark and red.

There was blood all over the sheets, pooled because the plastic mattress protector had stopped it soaking in. There was blood on Miss Spindleberry's lips. Beside her lay a shattered Appalachian harp.

"I broke it over his head," she whispered. "When he knifed me, I knew what I had to do."

"Lie still, be quiet," said Nurse. "I'll get an ambulance."

There was a bubbling noise in Miss Spindleberry's throat. "No. Let me go. I have sinned. I took Boy's knife and said, 'Right you little bastard. If you're so damned hungry, eat this.' Then I cut his little willy off and shoved it down his throat. I didn't think he would bleed so much." She coughed and blood poured from her mouth.

The nurse felt sick. The small incision in the chest of Miss Spindleberry had done more injury internally than had been immediately apparent. It had certainly ended her days of earthly misery.

Boy's eyes had rolled up. She took the terrible thing from his mouth and he gasped for breath. Brenda ignored him. She fetched a sheet from the linen cupboard, soaked it under the shower and laid it on the floor. The plastic shower curtain was placed on top of it. When Boy stopped writhing, she lifted the child onto the floor and rolled him into the sheets so that he was cocooned as if in swaddling clothes.

Jennifer Kingsbury, who had followed her into the room, had slumped to the floor and watched the nurse in mute horror. Brenda Jones was grateful. She had no time for hysteria. She closed the wound in the mother's chest with strips of tape.

"Get a bowl of water and clean Miss Spindleberry," she ordered. "I'll strip the bed and burn the linen. You get clean sheets and a fresh nightdress."

"Why? Why are we doing this?" asked Jennifer Kingsbury. "Why aren't we just calling the police?"

Nurse Brenda told her. "What's happened here is not natural. You want reporters swarming all over Barking Creek and tourists coming to gawp at us?"

An hour later Doctor Badgery, still in his dressing gown, was brought from the nursing home. He was more confused than usual.

He was ushered into a room where a dead woman lay, on clean linen, the top sheet drawn up over her bloodless features. The nurse drew it back so he could see that it was indeed Miss Spindleberry.

"Natural causes, you said?" His voice quavered.

"Natural causes. She had cancer. Just sign the death certificate, there's a good man. Then I'll take you home."

Boy, in the spare room, made no sound. He looked fast asleep. He had been given an injection of pethidine that would have knocked out an elephant.

"Better he doesn't wake up," the nurse told Jennifer Kingsbury. "It'll not be long. Now, you know what must be done? Pass the word."

*

They came for Boy in the half dark before dawn. There were almost a hundred people from Barking Creek, population 314. All wore large green plastic garbage bags over heads and shoulders, with eye-holes cut in one side. Each carried a cloakroom ticket, provided by Mrs Marker from the shop. They picked up Boy and carried him on a litter down the main road to the churchyard. He was set down in the church porch, as near to hallowed ground as anyone dared take him. No one saw who laid the silver knife next to him. It was the silver knife that had cut a hundred wedding cakes in Barking Creek.

No one said a word as the bucket used for chook raffles was held out and a ticket drawn from it. "Red 94," said a voice that trembled. There was movement at the back of the crowd. A tall figure stepped forward, took the handle in a trembling hand.

"I can't do this," said the man who some thought might have

been the father.

"Nonsense," said Nurse Jones. Plastic bags cannot disguise voices. "He can't feel a thing. He's long gone."

Gerald the lecher plunged the blade into Boy's body. There was a deathly hush.

"Do I leave it there?" he asked, hand still on the knife.

"Yes. Leave it. We don't want his spirit lurking."

*

Later that morning a hundred townsfolk, dressed in black, followed the undertaker's hearse to the hastily dug grave in the churchyard. They sighed as the preacher read the funeral service and Miss Spindleberry's coffin was lowered into the ground. Ashes to ashes, dust to dust. She was blessed and her body consigned to the care of Almighty God.

As was that of her son, who had been buried earlier at the bottom of her grave. He had then been covered with Holy Water and earth in the pale light of a brand new day.

"Rest in Peace," said Ted Kingsbury, and threw up on the War Memorial.

Rough Justice

"Pioneer's cottage, circa 1800," said Charles Wright. "Modernised. Vacant possession. Furnished."

"I don't like it," said Prunella. "It looks as if nobody's loved it for a hundred years."

"Let's look." Charles waved the keys. It was his idea to buy a country property from the proceeds of his last best-seller. Prunella wanted an apartment at Noosa where the surf was high and the social life cruisy. She said so.

"Impossible. Marcus hates the beach. Salt water gives him eczema. He'd love it here."

"Damn Marcus. And this place. My mobile won't work." Pru was trying to contact her Brisbane agent about a part in a TV commercial.

"It's a mobile dead spot. I expect it's the Cunningham Range."

"It's the dead end of civilisation!" she snapped.

Charles sighed. "Diggerty's has got an ordinary phone. Look, I need quiet if I'm to finish my new novel on time. Come on, Pru, it isn't far from Brisbane. I can have a bedroom for a study and still leave a spare for guests."

An early morning shower had left droplets on the window panes. The water was trickling like tears onto the sill. Pru pointed this out. "This is a miserable place!"

"Weep no more," Charles murmured to the cottage. "We'll care for you." He turned the key. As if hypnotised, Pru followed him.

The door creaked like old boat-timbers rubbing against a

jetty, the sigh of something tethered, longing to be free.

"No damp course," said Pru, sniffing. "The place is musty."

"You'd be musty if you'd been neglected for nine months."

To the right was a dining room, a pleasant space with walnut furniture masked by a thick layer of dust. Cobwebs covered an ornate crystal chandelier.

"Bad taste," said Charles. "Sticking a glittering monstrosity on a pioneer ceiling. It goes!"

"We'll fix the drains first. Something's on the nose."

"Squirt that stuff you put under your arms."

The sitting room was dominated by a huge fireplace in which ashes lay, grey and unwelcoming. A nasty draught from the chimney stirred the flakes. Pru shivered.

"Why no dust sheets?" she grumbled. "It'll take weeks to get this place fit to live in."

"We'll get cleaners in," her husband promised. "Maybe get you a daily help if I get a good advance on Shenandoah's Darling."

"If the kitchen's worse than this, you'll need one, because I won't be living here!"

To her surprise, the heart of the house was brilliant, stylish units in American oak, an ultra-modern stove and a dishwasher. There was a gleaming refrigerator with an icemaker in the door, next to a large freezer. She reeled back when she opened it. The stench was appalling.

"I should have warned you," Charles said. "The owners forgot to empty it when they left in a hurry. Everything was off before the agent noticed it. He said they buried the contents in the garden but hadn't been able to get anyone prepared to scrub it out."

"Don't look at me! You can do it. You have a terrible sense of smell. You can't even tell when Marcus needs a bath."

Charles grinned. "One nose is enough. I need yours, darling." He drew her close. "Come on, Pru. This is the nicest place we've seen."

"It isn't, but it's the only one in our price range," she sighed. "Oh, very well."

*

"You're the young couple who bought Diggerty's?" asked the local shopkeeper. "Awful mess it was in, I hear from the Warwick cleaners. You'll not get any one round here to do for you. Folks don't like Diggerty's. No one stays there for long. You planning on settling?"

"We like it. I'm a writer. Wright the writer. Joke."

The shopkeeper sniffed disdainfully. "Writers had it before the war. Mind you, there was no trouble at Diggerty's until they moved in. Very peculiar gentlemen they were, if you gets my meaning. Unnatural. You know?"

Charles gave a stiff smile. Homophobia was alive and kicking in rural Queensland. "We'll try to find a regular help from town, then. There's a bus service, isn't there?"

"There is, but whether a daily would stay, that's another matter."

"Perhaps there's someone who'd do the garden?"

"Terry Poacher might. He was in the army and he don't scare easy. Only got one good leg, but it's wonderful how he can dig. Talks funny but he's all there. I'll send him round. Now, is that all?"

Charles looked at the shopping list. "Yes. No. We've forgotten the dog food."

"You've never brought a dog to Diggerty's, have you?" The shopkeeper shook her head. "They ought to have told you. Dogs and Diggerty's don't mix."

*

Marcus was relieved to see dogfood. He didn't like car travel. It usually meant the vets or a week or so in a boarding kennel. He didn't like moving. He was too old for change. He was going grey around the muzzle and was rather deaf.

Charles was following the removal van which had been at the Brisbane apartment. Marcus hoped his basket was in the van. Now the master had stocked up on supplies, he suspected food was not far away, wherever that might be. He sat up and panted down the back of his master's neck.

They turned onto a narrow track towards the ranges. There was the scent of kangaroo and rabbit in the air. The removal van was parked outside a low stone cottage in a wild garden. Beyond was a tangle of undergrowth fringing a pocket of rainforest. It seemed a place where a dog could wuffle to his heart's content.

When master opened the car door Marcus leapt out and ran madly round and round the garden, nuzzling this and that, marking his territory, barking with excitement because he could smell something wonderful buried at the end of the vegetable patch. It ponged of long dead meat. Master filled his drinking bowl. Marcus lapped thirstily, flopped down and lay panting in the sunshine, contented with the new environment.

*

The removalists unpacked boxes and stowed the contents away as instructed. They were not happy. By the time the sun was curtsying to the horizon, all was shipshape. The men nervously assured Charles they could move him again in a hurry, at a price.

Water and power were connected and the gas bottle was

full. Prunella said the cleaners had been thorough. She made the bed and arranged bowls of fresh flowers. She took two gourmet meals from the new freezer and popped them in the microwave. Charles lit a roaring fire, for the night was turning cold. He opened Meatychomp for Marcus.

"Din-dins!" he shouted, standing at the door. There was no response. He tapped the metal bowl with a spoon.

Marcus said "Ruff!" but refused to budge.

"Come on, old fellow. Come into the warm." Charles patted Marcus, took his collar and led him towards the doorway. Marcus, stiff-legged, growled. Charles straddled the dog's back and lifted, half-dragging him up the steps. The hackles on the retriever's neck rose and he started barking, wriggling to get free, but his master kicked the door shut behind them. "Silly bugger," Charles said affectionately. "Eat your dinner."

*

"Think of me as Catastrophe," spat the big black tom. "Get this straight. I hate most men, I despise women and I loathe dogs. This is my place and I am the boss. Got that, mutt?"

The cat yawned and dabbed a paw towards the bowl of beef and gravy. He padded closer, sniffed at the food and pretended to lick it. "Smells good, looks good. Pity I can't use it."

Marcus growled menacingly and bared his teeth. He did not like cats, not even ones which were faint and misty. He could see right through this one to his basket, placed by the stove which kept the water hot. He kept his eyes on the apparition while he gobbled his meal. So, the feline ghost couldn't use food? Cats invariably lied. Toms not only lied, they were devious and manipulative. This he knew. He licked the bowl clean and growled again.

"Have you noticed that Marcus won't look at his food?" said

Charles. "He's got his eyes on something else. Can't think what."

"It's only natural he should be taking in the surroundings," said Prunella. "Carry your tray to the sitting room. It's too cold to eat in the dining room. There's a chill in the air."

Marcus eyed his basket. He badly wanted to test it, to find out if it was a cosy spot. The cat hunched a shoulder and sidled across to the wickerwork bed. Catastrophe stepped daintily in and curled up, washing each paw carefully before closing slanted eyes. The phantom paid no attention when Marcus put his head down and barked furiously. "Ruff! Ruff! Ruff!"

A lazy claw scratched his nose. Catastrophe narrowed his green eyes to a slit. "I can hurt you, mutthead. There'll be no blood, no mark, but you'll feel as if there is. I have the power. No, don't try to bite me. I'm not here in the physical sense, you dumb pooch. Material bites material; ectoplasmic bites ectoplasmic. Surely you know that, Goofy? All you'll bite is your own sloppy tongue."

"Stuff that," thought Marcus and bit anyway. He reeled around the room trying to get a feline jawful, bumping into the furniture, overturning the waste bin.

"The dog's gone mad," screamed Prunella, knocked off balance while taking trays to the sink. Dinner plates shattered. Forks and knives clattered.

Charles dragged Marcus to his basket and tied him to the table. Catastrophe, leering, danced around on the hot surface of the stove and said, "Tee hee! Want to see my powers?"

The only response was a low grrrr. The tom rose in the air and appeared to fly around the room like a bird.

"See? No flap. Good, isn't it? And for my next trick, believe this, puppy dog, I am the greatest!" Catastrophe doubled his size, and again, and again, and again. The walls shook. Plaster fell from the ceiling.

Prunella screamed, "Earthquake!"

The lights went out.

"Damn!" Charles found matches and lit a candle. "Leave everything, darling. It's only a power cut. Let's go to bed."

Marcus started barking and whining. "Oh, for God's sake bring him to our room or he'll have us up all night," Prunella sighed.

The fire went out. The stove went out. Catastrophe, who was a sucker for comfort, got back into the dog basket and slept.

*

Marcus found a sympathetic ear in Terry, the gardener. The shell which had taken off the former soldier's leg, during a training exercise in Townsville, had also affected his speech. However, he had the sight. He could see Catastrophe but, having survived an army one, wasn't about to be spooked by a cat with nine lives scratched. Terry wore his grandmother's cross when he came to Diggerty's.

He understood Marcus. He found the old dog trying to excavate the buried meat from the freezer. Marcus badly wanted to roll in it because he reckoned the dead tom would leave him alone if he stunk.

"Dogs that pong get the chop," the gardener said, stumble-tongued, scratching Marcus's back just in the spot he could never reach. "You don't want to be put down, do you? Let's dig potatoes instead."

Terry was good company. He told Marcus about Cedric and Horace, who lived at Diggerty's before the war. "They were Satanists," he said. "Bad, black-hearted buggers." He explained that Catastrophe had been Cedric's familiar.

"After the two old queers died...poison it was...some said a suicide pact but my granny reckons the devil took his own...the damned cat starved. My granny used to bring it food, but it wouldn't have a bar of anything touched by a Christian hand. It lived off wild rabbits until it was snared and choked to death."

The dog whined and panted in approval. "Ruff. Damn good thing. Ruff!"

Terry shared his sandwiches with Marcus. He refused to step into the kitchen for tea but asked Prunella to put his brew on the doorstep.

"Better I eat in the toolshed," Terry mumbled. Marcus thought the shed was as good a retreat as any.

The old dog didn't like the smell in the house. Catastrophe had, among other powers, retained the ability to spray. Ghostly glands were no less powerful than the mark of a tom in musk. Not only did the cat leave his calling card on Marcus's food dish, in his basket and on his favourite hearth rug in front of the fire, but also sprayed on Prunella's side of the bed and in her wardrobe.

"This place stinks of cat's piss and it's no good you telling me it's the flowering currants in the garden because they're out of season." Prunella ranted at Charles who, deep in the action of Shenadoah's Darling, barely noticed her existence most of the time. She started taking long walks with the dog to get a breath of fresh air.

She got no welcome in Warwick. The locals crossed themselves as she passed in case, her being tainted by proximity with evil, she could cast an eye on them and theirs. Marcus enjoyed the excursions and understood what the mistress was going through. He told Terry about it, in so many ruffs.

"You've got trouble comin'," Terry warned. "That black devil will have the missus out of here first. He'll call his Lord to come acourtin' Mrs Wright. There's no man as can pleasure a woman like the Black Lord."

And so it was. Charles, working late on his book, slept on the couch. Prunella came languorous to the breakfast table, called him wonderful and a divine lover. Charles, who agreed, was surprised his wife remembered the last time they'd been intimate.

It was several weeks before he woke with indigestion and heard the unmistakable noises of passion coming from their room. He threw open the door to find her alone but writhing in ecstasy. He readily obliged but wondered what drugs she was on.

Catastrophe went wild when he realised that, far from driving out the woman, she was enjoying the attention of the Dark Lord. He turned wicked. Charles had reluctantly agreed to take dinner with his wife every night. He had, she said, to eat at least one proper meal a day, and she had a right to his exclusive attention for a few hours. Shenandoah could be her own darling for a short period. She prepared delicious meals, put lace cloths and crystal goblets on the table, arranged low bowls of flowers and sprayed her neck with the perfumes of Araby. She dressed to entice and Charles was enchanted.

Marcus watched the cat show with alarm. He could see Catastrophe levitating to the ceiling, patting the droplets on the chandelier until they tinkled wildly. The first night's sporadic jangles were enough to cause only mild alarm. The cat grinned and ceased.

"We should replace that fitment," Charles said. "I always said it ought to go."

It took ten dinners of increasing disturbance before the whole light came down in a shower of cut glass and spaghetti marinara. On the eleventh night the Wrights dined by candlelight, no electrician being available for three days. Charles had turned off the mains and cut the offending debris free, sealing off the live wires with insulating tape as instructed by telephone.

That night the wine bottles defied gravity. They fell over, no matter which way or where they were stood. The sauterne dribbled onto Prunella's blue silk; the claret soaked Charles. Marcus licked up the Chivas Regal. He was dog drunk.

When the poltergeist phenomena increased, Charles agreed there was something odd about the house. Catastrophe raced around unseen, knocking ornaments to the ground, tipping pictures askew, throwing cushions and flicking burning coals out of the grate. The Wrights were frightened and bewildered. Marcus told Terry about the beastly mog and Terry got the vicar to intervene.

Diggerty's was exorcised. Getting rid of incubi and succubi did nothing except ruin Prunella's sex life. The Dark Lord scratched her name from his appointment book. The cat laughed, claiming church rituals did not cover felines.

Marcus, increasingly stressed, developed kidney trouble. He got his own back on his tormentor by piddling where Catastrophe liked to sleep. It was a successful strategy until Prunella caught him cocking his leg against Charles's fireside chair.

"That is IT!" she shouted. "Take him to the vet. He goes or I go!"

Marcus knew the word vet meant injections. He didn't know this was his last. Charles cried, with a paw in his hand, as Marcus passed over the great clichéd divide to the happy hunting ground.

The spirit of Marcus rode beside the author as he returned to Diggerty's. The dog felt active, empowered, ready to fight the good fight. He walked through the car door after Charles locked it and passed easily through the wall into the kitchen.

Catastrophe was in the basket. Marcus bared his fangs and gave a silent growl. Then he bit, deep into the jugular. There was a startled caterwaul and, spraying invisible blood, the tom bolted through the back door and into the forest, the ghost of Marcus in cold pursuit. Ectoplasm hunted ectoplasm. The dog won.

*

Charles, sitting in the garden with Terry, with whom he'd reached an understanding, autographed a copy of Shenadoah's Darling for the gardener. The book was dedicated. 'To Marcus, strong in spirit, who saved us from catastrophe.'

Pru, very pregnant, poured the beer. "I miss the dog, you know."

Charles smiled. "Me too, but I often think I smell a whiff of him. His memory lingers, you see."

Terry glanced at the vegetable patch, where the ghost of Marcus was in seventh doggie heaven, rolling in the dirt above the place of the dead meat.

"You dirty bugger," Terry muttered to himself. "It's a good job the master can't see you."

"Ruff," said Marcus. "Ruff! Ruff!"

Touch Me, Hold Me

When the shadows started rolling in, like a line of dark storm clouds seen on the horizon, what little remained of my sight was lost to me. Before the front arrived there had been a wispy mist which dulled vision, which made highlights and deep blues and blacks meld into shades of grey. Colours lost their intensity and edges their sharp definition.

I knew what was happening. It was no surprise. Specialists had been warning for years of the impending atrophy of my sight. I rejoiced that I had been given the privilege of seeing the world before it was lost to me. Though hampered by spectacles with increasingly thick and distorting lenses, I had taken note carefully, storing pictures in my mind to sustain me in the future.

How odd it was, I reflected, that they who would be able to see clearly into old age, observed so little. I would look in wonder at a shell, at each whorl and striation, marvelling at its colour, its gloss, the complex marks of muscles where its internal organs had been attached, or the byssus by which it might have clung to the sea floor. How many hours did I spend studying flowers, their structure and shape, the texture of petal and calyx, their scent and the taste of the sap exuding from the stem. Feathers were a marvel. By the time I was in my teenage years I knew what species each feather came from and the part of the bird's anatomy from which it had fallen.

Yet, all the time my eyes were active, so were my fingers. I taught them to see whatever they could touch. Only colour was missing but there a supersensitive nose helped. There was a minutely different scent to yellow objects, to those which were red, or blue, or purple. Much was to do with their chemical composition. How easy it was to distinguish between pale ochres and other earth colours, such as Indian red or burnt sienna, and those based on tannins. Knowing that the need would soon be there, I tuned all my senses to compensate for sight.

Those early years gave me the framework on which I could build, the skeleton which I could flesh, the map which my mind could follow.

I had already learned Braille by the time the printed word faded into a blur. I had committed to memory my favourite sheet music and could play the piano and violin with some artistry. My ear was true and new tunes were quickly learned. I had, indeed, been blessed with intelligence and total recall.

I had also been granted the great joy of warm parental love. My mother, who was a woman of hugs and kisses, said that I was gifted. My father, more given to the pat on the shoulder or the affectionate squeeze of my hand, sighed a great deal. I had been a late-born son, making an appearance when hope of a family had all but disappeared. Father, older by ten years than Mother, worried what would become of me. He worked long and hard to ensure we would both be financially secure when he passed on.

Mother, who had been devastated at first to learn of my condition, made sure my emotional well was full. She gave to us, not only happiness, but a philosophy which enabled us to face adversity with hope and determination.

It was she who persuaded Father to buy a small house near the centre of town while I could see well enough to memorise the streets, the buildings, the ways to get to the sea and the harbour, the parks and the shops I would one day need. She walked them with me, standing patiently while I placed my hands on brick and mortar-jointed masonry, learning the modern materials from those used by Federation builders and the convict gangs. When the dark days came, I could walk the port city with confidence. I knew the history of every place around the town centre and the feel of the pavements underfoot.

"You'll need to look after David when we're gone," she told the mayor. "You may as well start now."

From that day on the council engineers would ring when any road works were planned, when pavements were to be bricked and square slabs replaced, when street sign post relocated and bollards place along the centre of the Terrace. If they planted trees or installed street furniture, a young council officer would meet me and walk me round the town so that changes were made to the street map in my head. It was a great kindness and one for which I was exceptionally grateful, especially as Mother died unexpectedly, only four years after I started carrying the white stick.

Oh, the sadness that enveloped our home. Father could not cope with the silence. We had not noticed how Mother had filled the rooms with the purr of her affection and how her voice, talking of commonplace events, had been as musical as the singing of a canary. I did not have the heart to play music. The piano gathered dust. The violin, which is a wonderful instrument for expressing heartbreak, knew not the caress of my bow. We listened to the radio but, after the news, Father would turn it off, muttering that never was there so much fuss about nothing. The television, which had been Mother's delight, was rarely used, except to watch Test Cricket. It was useless to me, without her kind female voice describing to me what was being shown on the unseen screen.

Father took to walking, long, energetic excursions on which I was unwelcome. I could not keep up with his rapid strides and his heedless rampage over uneven surfaces. He walked at night and, while time of day made little difference to me, I understood his need to be alone to cry out his grief to wind, wave and the silently wheeling gulls. He tramped in misery past the prison to Monument Hill and, I was told, stood four-square to the wind and moaned, "Come back, come back."

Neither rain nor cutting winds from the Antarctic could stop his regular visits to the cemetery, which was several miles from our home, along a busy highway past the golf course. Sometimes he would follow the footpath past the houses, sometimes meander along the wide grassy verge on the side which lay below the fairways. Was it tears which blinded him on the night he chose to walk along the gutter?

"I didn't see him," said the truckie, ashen-faced. "It was sheeting down with rain and I was having trouble seeing the road ahead. I wasn't expecting to see anyone out walking. It was nearly midnight, for Pete's sake. One minute he wasn't there, the next he was. I couldn't do a blind thing about it, officer. I just slammed on the brakes and look where that ended me. In some poor bleeder's front garden."

Shock stilled my tears until after the funeral. It was well-attended. A friend of the family told me who was present and many people came to me to express their regrets at Father's death. Many had also offered condolences at Mother's burial, but it was interesting how different were the mourners. The core was the same, friends and family but, while Mother's had drawn in those who had shared her artistic interests and voluntary work, Father's were civic dignitaries and business colleagues.

Present at both was Helen, the council engineering assistant, who had been my guide to changes in the streetscape for several years. She laid her hand on my arm and I knew her touch.

"I'm so sorry," she whispered. Then her hand came up and touched my cheek. She drew my face down to hers and kissed me softly. "David, I am so terribly sorry."

Tears came unbidden and I fumbled for my handkerchief. Others had given sympathy. She was the only one who sounded as if she truly cared. I was unmanned by this small token of affection.

"Can I do anything to help?" she asked, hesitantly.

I flapped my hands and snuffled, uncoordinated, uncaring if anyone looked at me. Most people had already left. The funeral director coughed and said he had collected the cards from those who had attended. He pressed them into my hand.

"I'll take those," Helen said. "Come on, David. I'll drive you home."

Not a word passed between us on that short trip, but it was a momentous journey. It was a journey from alone to not alone. I took my stick from her when she had parked a little way down the road from our house, and tapped along the boundary walls of neighbouring properties until I came to our front gate. Helen took the door key from my trembling fingers and let herself inside. By the time I had settled myself at the kitchen table and given way to great howls of misery, she had boiled the kettle and brewed a stiff pot of tea.

I blubbed myself dry and didn't care whether I was making a fool of myself. It wasn't simply sorrow which had gushed out like an erupting volcano, it was fear.

"What shall I do? What shall I do?" I repeated, twisting the condolence cards in my hands.

"Give them to me," she said, putting a mug of hot sweet tea into my shaking fist. "I'll write letters to them. You can't do it, after all."

I shook my head and was comforted. Helen read the cards and told me who had been there. She described the floral offerings to me and told me what colour my wreath had been. She had a soft and pretty voice and a way of expressing things which was clear yet sensitive.

"I've known you for how long? Five or six years, David? I

never knew you were a music lover," she said. "Do you play the piano or was it your mother's?"

"I play," I said, steadying myself. "But not recently. Father couldn't bear any music after Mother died and, to be honest, I didn't have the heart for it either."

"That's sad. Music is such a balm to the soul. It says what words cannot. Play for me, David, please."

How many hours I spent at the keyboard I do not know. It might have been most of the evening, but I knew when she left. I heard her pottering around in the kitchen. "I've made sandwiches for your supper," she murmured, smoothing a lock of hair off my forehead. "No, don't stop playing. I enjoy that fugue."

I heard her open and close the front door and the sound of her little car driving away. The scent of her perfume lingered. Whenever I smell jasmine I think of Helen.

She came back. In fact, she never really went away again. She returned with the letters for me to sign. She helped me sort out my Father's business affairs. She taught me to cook and laughed when I burned things. She walked with me to listen to music at the Arts Centre, introduced me to ethnic music in a cultural Mecca above the street where the interesting folk of the town gathered for coffee and conversation.

I had not been out many times at night. It was not because I had been afraid to do so or that I shunned company. Rather it was because home was so complete and my parents' company so warm and satisfying, that I had no need of more. Now there was a void and Helen showed me how to fill it. My sensory horizons expanded. I became filled with new experiences, new sounds, new tastes, new perfumes. Gradually, imperceptibly, I became filled with Helen. Soon I realised that she alone could people my world. I needed no one else.

"If you could see me, you wouldn't call me beautiful," she murmured, when she recovered from my first tentative proposal. I kissed her, my fingers eager to learn her features by touch, to drink deeply of her scent, to feel the texture of her hair, her skin. I knew the timbre of her voice, the quality of her mind, the kindness of her heart. She was shy. She had loved and been hurt. I knew she feared rejection and she had resigned herself to solitude for she was not young and had arranged her life as spinsters do, in self-sufficiency.

I was humbled by her affection, by the sacrifices she made in taking on a burden, which was how I saw myself, and was grateful when she agreed to marry me. I knew by then that she was greying, for there is a coarseness in hair which has lost its first colour. I knew that she was plump and ashamed of her stocky figure. My fingers told me her nose was snub and her skin had been scarred by acne in her youth. Her mouth was too wide and her eyes had smile lines around them. My fingers found the marks of the frown of worry between her brows.

To me she was beautiful and I told her so. She was never more lovely than when she gave herself to me, shyly at first, then, as her body came to know the sensitivity of my fingers and the size of my desire, in generous measure, in lusty heartiness, in playful, laughing unity.

Ah, Helen, I loved you then and through the passing years.

Our only sadness was that mine were the only lips to suckle, mine the only body to emerge from her loins. There were to be no children of our love yet she did not pine for them. Perhaps I was all the child she needed, just as I was all the man she ever dreamed of, or so she said.

I loved her when her hair grew thin and the skin on her neck grew crepey, when her cheeks sagged and there were whiskers on her chin. I said she was still beautiful when her breasts sagged and her poor hips ached with arthritis. I was gentle with her but still we loved. We loved with a great intensity, for she was fifteen years my senior and had her first heart attack when she was only sixty-two.

"Don't stop," she'd say, "This is the way I'd like to die, locked in your arms, David."

I made love to her even when my vigour faded, for I knew that I was imposing on her fragility and my body would not rise to my inner urgency. There were, however, other ways to love and my fingers were our friends. There came a time when the greatest intimacy she could bear was to put our dentures in a glass and shake them round together with pink fizzy cleanser.

We laughed at the joke. Gentle humour sustained our hearts. Then she was gone.

No, I'll not dwell on the emotional distress that Helen left behind her. Only I need recall the wilderness years, the utter desolation of being one and all alone again. Sorrow might have ridden, baying, on my heels for years, but I was selected to have a guide dog.

Cindy was my salvation. I had someone to care for once more, and someone to care for me. I had become a recluse after Helen's death. Now I ventured into the world again. I took up music once more and went out and about where those of good heart gathered. I could look back on the Helen years with joy and with gratitude.

I was only in my early sixties. I was fit. I was healthy. I was, God damn it, virile. I had led an active and wonderful sexual life for more than thirty years, though I had reigned in my desire in the latter period. I did not seek another wife, nor even a permanent relationship. Helen was irreplaceable. She had all of my heart and I could not imagine loving another. Love does not equate with sex.

Instead I found Pompadours. Cindy knows the way to that place of physical delight. We visit once a month, for that is all my limited income will permit. They are kind to me there, the girls. They let me love them mightily and, as I did with my darling Helen, I make sure they are pleasured also.

They do not get much love, the girls of Pompadours. They are beautiful, with their high, hard jutting breasts, their narrow, lissom waists, their firm and agile hips. There is Su Ling, tiny and oriental, a fragile handful; Lotte, who tells me she is blonde and comes from Denmark; Annabelle, who smells of musk and the dark chocolate of New Orleans, and Pixie, from Ireland, who is the wickedest romp imaginable.

I love them all, in small measure. My hands have known all that young rubbery resilience, all that pert thrust of engorged nipple, and those inquisitive fingers on my flesh.

But how can I tell them that I yearn for breasts grown soft and flaccid, for broad hips and sagging belly, for double chin and wrinkly neck, for hands whose knuckles are swollen with age?

They sometimes cry when it is over. I know this, because I can taste the tears on their cheeks. They say they cry because I have made them happy, because I have given them love which has made them feel special.

They never ask me why I cry, and I could never tell them.

An Independent Cuss

"See that?" said the magnate, pointing at an area of high mineralisation photographed by a sophisticated satellite. "If that's not gold, I'm a monkey's uncle!"

The cattle-cocky looked at the detailed geological maps covering the same area. He was pretty familiar with the surface features of the Parra gold-field. His pastoral station ran as far south as the old ghost town which had been built at the time of the 1890s rush. James McHendry had ridden the boundaries of Muddee Creek five hundred times or more by horse and on a motor bike. In recent years arthritis had kept him out of the saddle but he could still drive his Landcruiser. He'd looked all over for signs of gold but had reached the conclusion that, when the great god Au was chucking it down, squeezing it into layers of quartz or filling the depths of the creek beds with mineral dust, he had given Muddee the go by.

So he drew deeply on the fine cigar and sipped the fine whiskey and eased his wrinkled old butt into the depths of the leather chair in the magnate's city suite. He hadn't minded being flown down for this meeting. James had enjoyed being wined and dined and treated like a fine fellow.

There wasn't much company at Muddee these days, not since the wife died. There wasn't much point in Muddee either, for Jim, the eldest boy, had died in Vietnam, the younger had become a doctor and worked in New York, and his only daughter was a kook who had married a missionary in Pogopogoland, wherever that might be. Nor was there much money in cattle after five years of drought and the cost of trucking bush steers to market. If this smart wheeler and dealer wanted to buy the station, he could have it. He'd probably pay more than could be asked on the open market, with a native title claim pending on the northern section and the Department of Aboriginal Affairs offering to pay $8 a square kilometre for the rest of the land so the Gugari people could run it.

"What's this got to do with me?" James McHendry said. "You want to buy Muddee? It's yours."

"Hell, no. We're into mining, not pastoral development." Gus Dreeman had an insatiable thirst for gold and what it could buy. "We've got mining leases over this entire area. Some we pegged ourselves, some we've bought from others. We've got government approval to drill and develop. What we want from you is this area here."

He stabbed a well-manicured finger at a small section near Parra Creek, lying under the ridge that ran south west from Muddee. "That's your land, and, as far as we can make out, you've pegged it. It's good country and we'll be generous."

McHendry sighed and squinted down the end of the cigar at the blue smoke curling from it. "You got it all wrong, mister. That's not part of Muddee. Sure, it was pegged by my son James and his partner, Larry Mungo, but after my boy died, Larry carried on working the prospect on his own. It was young James's wish that I make part of the lease over to his mate, so I did. It's all done legal, like. You see, Larry needed a place of his own after Vietnam. He didn't come back the same as when he went. And my boy didn't recover from his wounds."

"We'd make it worth his while to sell," the magnate said. "We'd not be able to work the deposit as an open cut with that small patch in the middle of the gold-field."

McHendry rolled his eyes and shifted his aching bones uneasily. "You'll have your work cut out, Mister. You've got sod all chance of shifting him. Larry Mungo is what you'd call an independent cuss!"

*

Home was an old boiler. It was one of the few remaining artifacts left in the ghost town. Stone walls had crumbled, timber frames had been eaten by white ants, and nearly all the corrugated iron that had roofed miners' huts or the drinking hole they'd called the Lucky Strike, had long ago been carted away for use as chook sheds, or whatever, in the nearest thing that passed for civilisation in the distant gold fields.

Larry hadn't been carted away, though he was as wrinkled as any rusted roof. In fact, when he leaned against the boiler, it was hard to tell metal from leather-brown hide. The digger was content with his lot. He'd had civilisation. The feeling was mutual.

He'd built a bit of a camp oven in the part of the boiler that had housed the fire-box. The big tank stood a foot off the ground, set on stone piers. It was a fair size and dry inside, but dark. The only light came from the inspection plate on the side, which served as entrance and window. Larry had hammered out every bolt but one, so that the plate swung open and could be propped up with a dead branch. It was an odd front door but he'd knocked up a bit of a ladder to make it easier to get in and out. At night he could pull on the rope to which it was attached as if it were a drawbridge. He was haunted by dreams of Viet Cong but would never admit it.

"There'll be no enemy troops in here, and no wrigglers either," he said to Dog, who lived under the boiler because he didn't have the legs for climbing. Dog did not mind snakes. This was not because he liked them. He was so darned stupid he didn't know they were dangerous. Dog was so stupid he didn't even realise that Larry was scared of the night, scared of the shadows and of what might lurk in them. Dog didn't like it when his man had nightmares. Those were the nights when the two of them would howl at the moon.

Dog was so stupid he didn't realise the man was very on the nose. Larry smelt good to him, most times, ripe and earthy. The lack of personal hygiene was not surprising because there was no water on the Parra field, other than a scummy pool in the creek. It was part of the daily ritual for the digger to fill a billy or two on his way back from his prospect each night. He kept an oil drum topped up, boiling it before drinking it with enough tea to ensure the tannin killed any bug lurking in it. It was there for tea and emergencies. It wasn't for washing. Oh, no!

Washing was something he did only when it rained. He dragged everything out of the boiler and draped it over mulga branches to let Hughie give it a quick rinse. He'd been known to strip naked and rub a bar of yellow soap over lean shanks and scrawny chest. He'd even work up a fine lather in his knotted hair if Hughie sent down a good soaker. If the rains didn't come he'd make do with a scrub down with dry sand if he got so much on the nose that even Dog wouldn't come near him.

There was better drinking water a day's hike away. Larry had an agreement with the cattle-cocky who ran Muddee Creek station. He kept an eye on the fencing in the southern paddock for Jim's old man. He made sure the windmill was still pumping artesian water to the cattle trough on Muddee flats. In exchange McHendry cashed Larry's pension and paid it into the account of an orphanage in Saigon. He also delivered supplies to the turn-off from the highway, some fifteen kilometres away. The rations, always paid for with a small bag of dust or a nugget or two, were left, as always, in the trunk of a burnt-out car, half hidden in the salt-bush, where it had come to rest after a tyre had blown out eight years earlier.

It was always the same order, cans of condensed milk, bully beef, tinned sausages and camp pie, strong English breakfast tea, a couple of loaves of bread, a can of ghee, because butter went off in the heat, a jar of golden syrup, half a kilo of cheese and one bag of apples and one of oranges. There were always potatoes, onions and carrots. Larry made a big pot of soup the day after the stuff was delivered and supped on it until it was so ripe he had to feed it to Dog, who was not forgotten. The order always mentioned a bag of dogfood. The digger also got two packets of rolling tobacco, papers, matches and a couple of bottles of cheap brandy.

On the seventh day of the week, marked by pebbles thrown daily into an old tin can, Larry dragged his only means of transport from the shade of the boiler. It was an old pushchair, the chrome peeling off and the canvas bodywork torn and filthy. The wheels were solid rubber and turned, although they were chewed by Dog and no longer circular. He dragged it behind him, fastened to a sort of harness he'd fashioned from leather straps. It was easy going down the narrow track that wound through mulga stands, over dunes thick with spiky spinifex grass, through pockets of deep bulldust and over the gibber stones of dry desert. It was hell coming back, for the pushchair had a mind of its own and wanted to go sideways when fully laden.

"It's enough to give you the proverbials," said Larry to Dog, who was too lazy to accompany him on his weekly foray for the rations. Dog used his morning off to hunt for kill left by wedge-tail eagles. He didn't mind carrion, even if over-ripe bones were all that was left for a good chew.

"Gawd, you smell 'orrible," said Larry. "Like a crapper. You stay downwind, mate."

Larry didn't order toilet paper because Jim's old man always left the previous week's newspapers for him to read. There was no sense of time on the Parra goldfield. Larry read the broadsheets cover to cover, then tore them up and hung them on a nail behind the dunny door. The dunny was a work of art. He'd salvaged four fairly solid sheets of corrugated for the sides and had bent a fifth into a half circle to roof the hut. Everything had been fixed onto a framework of two by fours with big roofing nails. The door hung on hinges made from fencing wire. There was a squat high partition below a solid wooden seat to make sure redback spiders didn't bite his legs. The seat had a comfortable manhole, under which he had placed a large plastic bucket which had once held chemicals. This could be reached from the back through an ingenious sliding hatch, once part of a sideboard found disintegrating in a disused weather station.

The dunny let in hordes of blue, busily buzzing blowflies and let out the pong. Once a week Larry would open the back and carry the malodorous bucket over the ridge which lay to the east, behind the camp and tip it down a shaft which some no-hoper had tried to dig in a bid to follow a vein of auriferous quartzite.

The digger, who knew fool's gold when he saw it, merely grinned when he found the shaft. He knew the good stuff was on the flank of the Parra breakaway, a sharp scarp below the main ridge, a two hours walk to the west. The alluvial stuff, which hadn't drifted far from the source because there wasn't much rain in those parts to wash it any significant distance, was long gone and, with it, the miners.

Only Larry and Jim had figured out that there was still gold in them thar hills. They'd had plenty of time to think about it in Vietnam. Without Jim, Larry, being lazy, had done no more than scratch at the surface of the strike, though they'd pegged the prospect fair and square and had the legal right to take what lay within the lease. Jim had wanted the world and had got sod all of it. Larry, in contrast, didn't want much. What he wanted, he wanted to own. He wouldn't buy a car, because he wouldn't buy on credit, he wouldn't buy a house, because he didn't believe in mortgages. He'd been there, done that, when he was a young man, before the draft got him. Once he'd had a woman, who'd sent him nearly bankrupt through hire purchase, in the days before credit cards became the rage. She'd run off while he was serving overseas and he'd said, "Good riddance."

Larry's patch could have enabled him to pile money in the bank, enough to buy anything he wanted but, to repeat, he didn't want much. He liked his life. The urge for wild living in the city grabbed him now and then. He'd scrub up properly, put on tidy clothes and gather his sack of pickings. Leaving Dog to fend for himself, he thumbed a lift to Kalgoorlie to sell the precious stuff. He had a haircut and a shave, spent the money on loose living, slow horses and fast women, got roaring drunk and, nursing a pounding hangover, emptied his pockets and his wallet into the first charity collecting tin he came to.

This time was no different from the last. Except for the correspondence. Larry settled his bills, and spoke to the bank manager about changing his donation to Saigon orphans to ones from East Timor as he'd just realised the little Aussie bastards left in Vietnam were now grown up and probably had kids of their own.

The offer from Gus Dreeman took him aback. He worried so much over it that he lost heavily at two-up. In the end he threw the letter in the bin and tried to forget it. He couldn't. Civilisation was making him antsy. He packed his swag and ambled over to the War Memorial to consult with Jim but it wasn't much help. The dead are not usually forthcoming. He leant back against the marble monument and rolled a couple of smokes and had a swig of brandy in Jim's memory, recalling the goddamn war and cursing the goddamn generals.

"You've not missed much, Jim," he muttered. He'd already explained about September 11 and the war with the ragheads. He'd tried to explain the fighting between Israel and Palestine but had given up on it. He'd reminded Jim it was the Queen's Jubilee year. "An' Ruth Cracknell's dead, an' all. You ain't missed a lot." He brightened. "But they said the Aussie cricket team was the best team in the world. Is that good, or what? I don"t suppose you care much, where you are."

Black-browed and dog-breathed, he struck out for home. There was a cattle truck heading north. The driver didn't mind Larry, for his days and nights were heavy with the pong of dung. The digger, after a few weeks in civilisation smelt relatively sweet.

*

There was a large sign at the turning to Parra, smelling of new paint. It said Parra Exploration United Inc. A wide road, oiled and graded, stretched away into the distance. A bulldozer had flattened the burnt-out car and had half-buried it under a windrow.

"Me booze! Me baccy!" Larry howled, jumping down from the truck cab. The driver got down for a pee and sighed in sympathy. He passed over a spade and watched as Larry shovelled the earth away from the trunk. "Some bastard has nicked my rations," the digger growled. "Bleedin' mongrels."

The driver passed him a pack of tailor-mades. "Best I can do, mate. See you some other time."

Larry felt as if the world had shifted in focus. He strode out, bewildered by the change to the landscape. The road was straight as a die, heading past the ruins towards the creek and due west into the sunset. To north and south a narrow track had been cut through the scrub and there were survey pegs everywhere. At 500 metre intervals there were signs of drilling, piles of samples laid out on a dirt pad, rock cores in neat trays waiting to be taken off for assay. He could see the rig ahead of him, working away, dust hanging above it and the roar of an engine driving the bit deep into the guts of the earth.

It had drilled right down the middle of what had been the main street. It had sunk a hole in the front bar of the Lucky Strike, knocking down a few walls to get to the spot. Now it was thumping away ten metres from his boiler. The drillers had a fire lit in his fireplace. One was on the rig. The other, goddamn it, was having a squat on his dunny, and with the door wide open. He was reading a copy of last December's Time magazine.

"What the eff are you doing?" yelled Larry. "That's my privy. You can't come bowling in here and use my dunger without so much as a by your leave. Bugger off!"

The driller grinned and wiped his butt on the cover page. "Says who?" He heaved himself up to a full six foot six; forget the metrics. The driller's shoulders filled the doorway.

"You bastards the one's who pinched my rations?"

"Nice brandy. You can keep the baccy. We don't use it. Stashed your other stuff under the boiler."

"Where's Dog?"

"Gone AWOL, mate, if you mean that stinking bag of bones. He don't like the rig and we don't like the barking. Made a ging and fired rocks at him until he snuck off. Could do the same for you, if you're a blurry nuisance."

Call Larry many things, but he had a brain cell or two, despite the brandy and the agent orange. He knew when he was facing an irresistible force. He needed to think and there was only one good place for that. He rolled a smoke and headed for the dunny. To his dismay, it was full to the brim. The drillers had made good use of it.

He sighed, opened the back hatch and gingerly dragged out the bucket. It was a long and unpleasant hike to the shaft he used as a midden. By the time he was halfway up the ridge he'd been joined by Dog, who'd been waiting in the scrub, hoping he'd return. He grunted a welcome and Dog rolled over to have his stomach scratched.

"Stupid mutt," Larry muttered, thankful to have someone to

talk things over with. He scrambled up the last rocks to crest the ridge and saw, to his dismay, that the whole area was a mining camp. There were transportable cabins everywhere, ablution blocks, mess hall, a workshop, a yard full of dozers and four-wheel-drives, and a mess of people milling around, building, hammering, shouting, marching off to vehicles with survey rods and theodolites. The area around his midden had been flattened. A large grader was parked over it.

"Well, bugger me!" said Larry, setting down his bucket of crap. "This place stinks of civilisation." He left the dunny waste on top of the hill and prayed that the pong would drift down to the intruders. He didn't need the bucket. He had a better idea.

He cleared out to his prospect for a couple of days, carrying only enough rations to see him through. He wanted to check his pegs were in place. He wanted to top up his piggy bank with nuggets and richly-veined quartz. He had a feeling the next few weeks would be expensive.

The drillers had moved on by the time he got back, leaving little piles of samples. They were working half a kilometre away. They'd crapped on the ground under the dunny, not caring that the bucket had gone.

"Pigs," said Larry, seizing a crowbar and loosening the iron pegs at each corner of his castle. He waited until after dark to move it into a new position. He took the cap off the drill hole and tested the vertical alignment of the dunny seat. There was a satisfying sound of silence. He didn't know how deep they'd bored and he didn't care. What he did know was that it was a long way down and it would take years for him to fill it.

Larry slept well that night, thankful to be back in the safety of the boiler. In the morning he shouldered his swag and his backpack of rock, and headed for the homestead at Muddee Creek. He stopped for a word with Jim, who was buried in the family graveyard overlooking the waterhole.

"I was wrong when I said nothing much was happening," he said. "All hell's let loose, mate. I think it's time to call in the heavy artillery. Now, what I want to know is, what was the name of that bloke who was a lawyer in civvy street? You know, the one that works for the Vietnam Vet's Association? Badger? Was that it? You think he'd call in a gunship for me?"

Larry thought Jim would approve of going down fighting. After all, they'd fought themselves out of trouble before, with everyone else dead and a Viet Cong mob storming up the hill towards them. They'd fought in retreat and, even though Jim had copped it in the groin, they'd taken out a few of the enemy before Larry'd had to put down his weapon and shoulder Jim instead, signalling desperately to be picked up and airlifted to base.

James McHendry had been expecting the independent cuss to turn up on his doorstep. "Why don't you sell out instead of fighting the miners? You'll not win the war," he predicted. "Gus Dreeman is a very determined and powerful man."

"We didn't win Vietnam, either," said Larry. "But we gave it our best shot. Now, can I use your phone or can I not?"

*

Two days later 'Badger' Button pulled into Parra, towing a luxury caravan behind the latest model all-terrain vehicle. There was a crowd of angry mining executives around the dunny, on which Larry was sitting, trousers around his ankles, holding a shotgun.

Badger, so named for his willingness to go down any hole a Viet Cong could dig, strolled across and confronted a man whose name-tag said Chief Geologist. "What seems to be the trouble," he asked quietly.

"This prad has built his dunny over our drillhole," the man

snapped. "And who the eff are you?"

"His lawyer. And you say you own the rights to this drillhole?"

"Parra Exploration has the mineral rights to this whole area. And the development approval to drill and mine. We can extract samples from all over the Parra goldfields."

Badger frowned. "I'm not arguing about that, but who says you own the hole? You've taken all the minerals and overburden out of it. All that's under that dunny is a couple of hundred metres of nothing but air. Show me your right to own air!"

The geologist was bright red in the face and almost jumping up and down with anger. Larry was grinning. "Nice one, Badger," he chuckled. "Now tell this ponce he don't have the right to drill here at all. This ain't on no mining lease."

"How do you make that out?" the lawyer asked, intrigued by the certainty with which Larry spoke.

"Because this here is a gazetted town-site. Been gazetted since 1894. You phone up the Department of Land Administration like I did last week. Their company has pulled a plonker."

Badger guffawed. "Nice one. But that doesn't mean you've got any claim to the land."

"So whose lawyer are you, mate? I've got every right to be just where I am."

"How do you make that out," snapped the geologist.

"It's called Squatters' Rights," Larry replied. "And I'm going to squat right here, on this dunny, until I fills up this damn hole."

"Your doing no good standing around here, shouting at my client," Badger pointed out to the Parra men, trying not to laugh. "Why don't you go and find out your legal position?"

When all was quiet Larry heaved up his overalls and came

across to shake Badger's hand. "Nice one, mate. I liked your opening shot."

"And I rather enjoyed your ground fire. That right about the town-site?"

"Blood oath. I don't go into a campaign without proper intelligence."

"Right. Now these are the tactics I think we should use." Badger was enjoying himself. It beat hell out of divorce cases and trying to get compensation for war veterans.

Larry made camp stew and they polished off a bottle of Bundi rum. The drillers had not realised there was anything inside the boiler as Larry had bolted it shut before he left for the city. They sat under a velvet sky and watched the stars do what stars do best - twinkle. They fought old battles, at ease with memories as only those who have shared them can be.

Day brought heavy hangovers and a need to give something back to Australia. The dunny got a warm seat. They could hear the distant sound of the drill and see the survey crews on the far horizon. They left Larry's ridge alone. He knew because he was watching them with binoculars.

"You struck it rich, over there?"

"Good enough," said Larry. "Have to be to afford your fees. You'll take them in kind? I don't carry much cash, out here."

Badger nodded. He liked the tax man no more than any other lawyer. He helped Larry stow several heavy bags in his caravan. Then he took his camera and started collecting the evidence he might need should matters come to court.

"You're a damn fool not to sell out," Badger said.

"Maybe, maybe not, but I figures that the harder I makes it, the more they'll want it."

The helicopter danced in at noon, landing as delicately as a dragonfly ready to lock on to a reluctant mate. Gus Dreeman himself stepped out, flanked by suits with briefcases.

"He's brought the legal beagles!" Badger was grinning. He knew them well. The legal world is so intimate as to be almost incestuous.

"You are getting right up my nose, Mr Mungo," the magnate said. "I want you out of here. You and your dunny. And your damned dog!"

"Hey, Mister. I thought you only wanted my prospect. Who said anything about getting rid of me altogether?"

"I could do that, too."

Badger raised an eyebrow. "Threats, Mr Dreeman? This isn't the way to go about things, surely?"

"I made a fair offer, a generous offer, but this independent cuss has completely ignored it."

"Peanuts," Larry drawled.

Badger scowled at him. "Mr Dreeman, Larry Mungo was twice decorated in Vietnam. He's got the Military Medal for bravery. He's not going to be cowed by your sort of bluster nor is he going to grab at your paltry offer to buy him off. Let me tell you what we've got planned for you. First there is the question of your company drilling on land for which you do not have drilling rights. Then there is the question of the destruction of a heritage building, the remains of the Lucky Strike Hotel."

"Don't forget the black-faced stick rats." Larry grinned. He'd invented the rare and endangered species only when the rum was in the bottom third of the bottle.

"And the black-faced stick rats. Then there is the question of Native Title. You did say there were petroglyphs on the ridge where your claim is, didn't you, Mr Mungo?"

"True enough," said Larry, touching a match to a tick on Dog's back. "Pecked out in the rock they are. Circles and things like the old Aboriginals made on Barrow Island. Of course, the archaeologists don't know about this lot."

"Yet," Badger added. He handed Dreeman a sealed envelope. "Our price! Now, why don't you go away and talk to your bean-counters, Mr Dreeman. Consult with your legal team."

Larry watched the helicopter as it lifted off and sank below the ridge. "Reminds me all the way," he muttered. "A chopper saved our lives, mine and Jim's."

"Mine too," said Badger, "Now get in the vehicle. We need to talk to James McHendry. And I need to use the phone."

The cattle-cocky found Larry in his usual place, sitting, yarning to Jim. "I come here too," he said. "Seems the boy is pretty close even though he's long gone." The old man swallowed the lump in his throat. "I don"t suppose you'd come and take his place at Muddee Creek? I'm getting old and I'm darned lonely of nights. I can't look after the station the way I used to, the way Jim would have wanted me to. And I don't like civilisation any more than you do, Larry."

"I'll think about it," said the independent cuss. "Thanks for the offer."

Badger's caravan stood where it had been left but Dreeman had not been idle. The bulldozers had flattened every wall still standing in Parra town-site. The stones had been pushed into the creek bed. The boiler, which had been rolled down to the embankment, lay on top of the rubble. The ground had been ripped and torn so that no foundations remained and no sign of the old roads could be seen. Only the dunny stood supreme, alone in corrugated splendour above the drill hole. Even the drill samples had been dozed.

"Keerist! He can't do that!" Larry gasped, appalled at the destruction.

Badger took his camera. "Ruthless bastard," he said. "We could ruin him with this."

"Yeah, man. Let's do it!" Larry was all fired up. "Let's crap on the bastard!"

The drillers, watching from behind rocks on the ridge, waited until Larry was within fifteen metres of the dunny before firing the charge under the seat.

"Whoomph," went the dunny, as it blew up.

"Whoomph," went Larry's sphincter, as it blew down.

Badger picked up his client and reeled back in dismay. He hitched up the caravan and passed out clean clothes and a jerry-can of water. "Make yourself decent," he barked. "We're going to pay Mr Dreeman a visit."

It is doubtful that Gus Dreeman had ever before been confronted with such fury and certainly never such legal arguments put with so much force.

It was not only environmental destruction to block a waterway but vandalism of a historic site, Badger said. Even more grievous was the explosion of the dunny, which had come close to attempted murder. The purchase price of the Mungo claim had just doubled.

"Make that treble," said Larry. "And throw in another half a mill for personal injury and mental distress."

Dreeman looked at the men in suits. They nodded. The magnate took out his cheque book and wrote out a fabulous sum, ending in many zeros.

"Thanks," said the independent cuss. "My lawyer here will

send you the papers to transfer the lease."

*

Nine months later James McHendry and his right hand man drove down to the southern boundary of Muddee Creek to watch the south-west ridge of Parra being fired.

It went up in a sequential explosion of brown and red and golden dust as the breakaway was shattered into fist-sized fragments. It was half a minute later before the crump, crump, crump of the blasts reached the ears of the watchers. Soon the trucks would move in to cart the ore to the crusher and the process of extracting gold from the ore would begin.

"Any regrets?" asked the old man.

Larry pulled back his shoulders and lifted his chin. "Not many. Jim would have approved. I don't need the money but I figured that in any war there's going to be widows and orphans of Australian soldiers who could make better use of it than Gus Dreeman. No, giving it to Legacy was the right thing to do. But..."

"But what, son?" said the cattle-cocky. "You said you'd no regrets."

"Only one, boss. I'd love to see Gus Dreeman's face when he finds out he's bought a pup. He was so eager to get his hands on my piece of the action that he didn't look closely at his own drill holes. The samples from under the dunny told the whole story. There's a fault under Parra Ridge. There's only ten metres of gold-bearing rock above the breakaway. I reckon the throw is several kilometres north-east. Right in the heart of Muddee Creek. You can't see the signs, but I know where it is."

The cattle-cocky put his arm around Larry's shoulder. "Let it lie, son. Let it lie."

Larry smiled and called Dog to his side. "Reckon you're right, boss. Jim can look after it until we're ready to make a monkey's uncle out of Dreeman for the second time."

A Burning Passion

Great bush fires swept the Blue Mountains like breaths out of the mouth of hell. A pall of smoke towered over the ranges, blue and billowing like some monstrous thunderhead. There was the smell of burning in the air. Tongues of flame licked the coast, forcing residents and visitors to evacuate by boat. Even in the cities there was ash in the air and the sun shone palely through the haze.

Every night television news showed firefighters, many from interstate, drooping with exhaustion, faces blackened with charcoal. Viewers saw the ravening fire wolves slavering across the national parks, snarling and tearing at the heavy understorey of dead leaves, bark and tangled scrub, leaping high into the tree-tops, which exploded as the volatile eucalypt oils caught fire.

Emergency workers dozed tracks in the path of the flames, bush-fire volunteers back-burned to stop the advance of destruction, only to stand helpless and bewildered as wildfire leapt the corridors of safety and rampaged on new fronts.

Unpredictable winds forced howling firestorms up narrow valleys and set fire to the flanks of escarpments on which homes had been built. The police ordered whole suburbs evacuated. Families in shock left their homes to the mercy of the fire and congregated in church halls and schools, some carrying overnight bags, others only such precious mementos as photographs or vital documents.

When the rains came and it was all over, some went home to houses saved by miracles, others to burnt-out shells and ashes of dreams. When it was over people took stock, especially those living in valleys which had escaped the disaster.

Brenda Bodanovic was among those stirred into action. "One of us should join the bush fire brigade," she said to Mirek. "You're no damn good, with your varicose veins and your high blood pressure. You should be the one to stay home here with the kids and the galah and keep the hose going on the roof. You be responsible for saving the family home and I'll go and learn how to fight fires."

If truth were told, Brenda was not only altruistic but maritally challenged. Mirek was ten years older and beginning to show it, in flab around the belly and a receding hairline. He worked hard in an insurance office but, although he was only a pen-pusher, he was exhausted every night. He ate then fell asleep in front of the television.

It had been easier when they lived in Parramatta but Brenda was country bred, from Glen Innes, and longed for a rural lifestyle. After a bequest from a great-aunt, she nagged until Mirek agreed to buy a place near Wentworth Falls, up in the Blue Mountains. He could commute by train, she said.

The house was her pride. It was perched on the top of a valley, overlooking a national park, always cobalt-tinged by the mist of eucalyptus in the air. She kept the windows sparkling clean so she could see the view. When she had finished she polished the wooden floorboards with wax until they gleamed. The house suited colonial antiques, so Brenda haunted auction sales and filled the home with good pieces which she cherished.

She planted azaleas and rhododendrons like those in gardens at Leura. She grew vegetables and grafted roses. It was full time work but, after the initial excitement, her days came to have a sameness which puzzled her. Everyday she'd rake the leaves from the trees around the property and wonder, was this it? Was this her lot? Married to a man who spent every weekend re-varnishing the cedar exterior of the house or mending windows which needed new putty? A man who needed vitamins?

The kids, Dulcie and Ormond, hated the place. They missed cinemas and coffee bars, youth clubs and amusement arcades. Even television reception was crook and Mirek refused to get Sky Channel. They were at the age when peer group pressure builds up a head of steam. It was explosively unfashionable to listen to parents. Brenda was torn between "Shut up!" to the sounds of sibling rivalry and "Wake up!" to the snoring, boring Mirek. Talking to the pet parrot was more rewarding.

It was stimulating, joining the volunteers. She enjoyed putting on her brightly coloured overalls, donning a hard hat, and learning how to handle reels of hose, to direct nozzles, to dribble fuel in the bush for back-burning. She didn't care if it was also back-aching, though it often was. She was the oldest of the women but they treated her no differently once they saw how keen she was and how fit. The flames, as they called themselves, formed a cheeky foil to the smokies, the larger group of men who, somewhat surprisingly, did not patronise them.

Except Nils. Nils was often teamed with Brenda because he was lean and skinny while she had the weight needed for certain tasks. He called her "My old flame," and sang snatches of the old song to her.

"My old flame, I can't even think of her name, but I wonder what became, of mi-eye oh-old flame!" Then he'd pinch her bottom. Or wink at her. That's as far as it went. He flirted with care. Brenda quite enjoyed the game. It was good to be appreciated, to see the twinkle in a man's eye, to realise that the possibility was there even if the probability was zilch. She was not, she told herself, a loose woman. She was not seeking an affair. Call her old-fashioned, but she'd remained faithful to her husband.

Her first two fire seasons were eventful but manageable. Mirek became used to her call to action, to his wife coming home weary and smoke-streaked. She looked forty on a good day, sixty after a fire. She was much trimmer, fit and firm. The kids looked at her with new respect. Dulcie persuaded her to tint her hair to hide the grey. Osmond got up on the roof and cleaned the gutters because she'd stressed how important this was should the house be under threat. Mirek put all important documents in the bank and stored the photo-albums in fire-proof boxes. He upped the insurance on the house to cover the antiques. He rigged the pool pump for use in an emergency. He went to the doctor and got a prescription for Viagra.

There came a wet summer when the bush burgeoned. Only a snake could have wriggled through thickets of brush choking the forest floors. There followed an unusually dry winter and a spring which brought no rain, only thirsty winds to suck moisture from the dying undergrowth.

The next summer brought drought and the levels in the dams fell. The bureaucrats started to talk about water restrictions. There were electric storms in the mountains but the winds from the dead centre blew the cumulus clouds out to sea. The fire hazard was extreme. Fire-spotters, high in their lookouts, directed crews to trouble spots. Lightning, being bloody-minded, struck places almost inaccessible to man and fire-tender. Most conflagrations were contained. It made good news coverage, being visually exciting as well as heroic - man fights nature.

Human nature being what it is, the fire-bugs crawled out. They struck in accessible places, only stopping briefly by the roadside to hurl burning firelighters into the forest. Being caught was on no arsonist's agenda.

And still the wind blew hot and dry and strong. It was relentless.

Even before the situation became critical Brenda was weary to the bone. When she did get home she slept in the spare room. No amount of showering could get the stench of smoke out of her hair. She did not want Mirek's arms around her. There was no comfort to be gained in his attention. All she wanted was sleep. Sometimes she'd roll into bed dirty and roll out ready for a quick coffee and a bite of toast before returning to duty. The family tippy-toed around her. Things were grim. The whole State knew that things were grim. All Australia held its breath, but the wind didn't.

Nils and Brenda were told to take an improvised water tanker to the fire front. Their route was along the crest of a ridge, on a dirt track. The crew was working five kilometres down the road. The need was urgent. Nils had his foot down. Smoke billowed from the valley to the north, thick, choking smoke that cut visibility down to zero. He didn't see the washout in the road and went into it with a lurch that rolled the tanker onto its side. Brenda was thrown against the quarter-light and whacked herself nearly senseless. Nils, who'd been strapped in tighter, had cut his forehead on the steering wheel and was slumped across her.

"Jesus!" He started there and went on to a full range of expletives. He pushed open the cab door, relieved to find that, though distorted, it hadn't jammed. He unbuckled his seat belt and, by standing on Brenda's hip, heaved himself from the vehicle. Then he reached in, cut her strap with a bowie knife, and hauled her out.

"Radio our position," Brenda gasped, trying to ignore the pain in her head.

"I tried," Nils replied, "But there's hell of a lot of crackling going on."

"That's not the radio, mate. That's fire. I reckon it's coming up the valley." She peered through the smoke to the gully to their north.

"Then we're in big trouble." Nils was on his feet, on the other side of the truck, wondering if he could winch it upright by anchoring the gear to a large redgum. "There's wildfire coming up from the south as well. Here, get up and give me a hand with the pump. The least we can do is drench the area around us."

It seemed a futile task. They dowsed the bush within a radius of ten metres before the pump coughed and choked to a halt. It whined helplessly as it drew in air.

"Effing thing!" Nils unclamped the manhole-size lid, which was normally on top of the tanker but was now within reach, and peered in. "There's still water in there, but the outlet's above the level."

Brenda felt like screaming. Behind them the flames from the gullies met and were howling like dervishes in the treetops. There was no escape that way. She turned and saw thick black smoke streaming towards them from the opposite direction. They were trapped.

"Get into the tanker!" Nils snapped. "Go on. Get in."

Brenda tried. Her overalls snagged on the catches.

"Take the bloody things off!" said Nils, stripping down to his underpants and throwing his protective garments into the water. Then he slithered through the hatch.

Brenda followed his example, cursing as her bra snagged. She unhooked it. She flattened her bosoms with her hands until they were past the lip. Then she squeezed into the dark cavity. Her hips stuck and she hung there, wriggling, in sheer panic. Nils grabbed her under the arms and heaved. She came free with a plop and fell into the water on top of her helper. It was a rugby scrum of naked flesh until they came up for air and found which bits belonged to whom. Then lips met lips and hands grew curious. Brenda whimpered as Nils pulled her close. They made love in a frenzied passion, doing anything, everything, to spit in the eye of death. They had no thought for consequences, only a desperate need for action rather than sitting in fear to await the inevitable. The fire wolves quarrelled along the ridge and pushed exploratory tongues into the hatch of the tanker, inhaling the very air. Brenda grew dizzy but had enough breath for a great scream of exultation and terror as both Nils and the fuel tank of the vehicle exploded.

"We're going to die!" Brenda wailed as Nils collapsed on her, unconsciously pushing her head into the water. She struggled free and heaved his head onto her lap, willing him to keep drawing breath, however lacking the atmosphere was in oxygen. "We're going to die!"

"If we go, we go together," he mumbled, gathering the energy to take her again as she grabbed his buttocks. "We die united!"

With that the giant helicopter flew overhead and dropped a thousand gallons of water on the smoking tanker.

"Holy spitting mackerel!" cried Nils, pulling out of Brenda with a jerk. "Get dressed! You think I want to be caught in a compromising position with you?"

"You turd!" Brenda gasped. "Me, compromise you? You forced yourself on me!"

"Didn't say no, did you? Mind, you're a pretty good lay for an old bag!"

"Why, you...you...you..." Words failed her. Suddenly she saw, with horror, what would have been said had their bodies been found, locked in the throes of a death passion. She knew she had been lucky - dead lucky.

She found her clothes and followed Nils out of the tanker hatch. Because she was wet with sweat she came out easier than she'd gone in. Maybe she'd even lost a couple of kilos on the hips through violent exercise. Who knows? She sat, tumbled and naked on the burnt out verge and felt ashamed.

"I bet Eve felt like this after that bloody serpent finished with her," she thought, watching Nils as he tucked his one-eyed trouser snake back into his dripping jocks. She put on her clammy underwear and struggled into the wet overalls.

Suddenly she felt very happy, almost exuberant, very much alive. She grinned at Nils. "Our secret, I think," she said, quizzing him.

"You bet. I'm a happily married man."

Brenda felt tears stinging her eyes and realised that, all in all, she had a good marriage, too. She wiped her face and streaked it with charred ash and dirt. She joined Nils, who was beating out small pockets of embers, stamping on them with boots that squelched. The sound of the chopper was heard in the distance. They gave it the thumbs up as it passed, watching as it dropped its next load in the gully down the road.

Within minutes the fire chief arrived in a tender. "We thought you two'd done a perish," he said, shaking their hands. "By damn, it was good to get the message from the water bomber that you'd come out of the fire-storm alive. How did you do it?"

Nils took him to the tanker and showed him the hatch. "Not a common design, but it saved our lives," he said. "We should adapt all the tankers to make them like this."

"Ah," said the chief. "Used to be a multi-purpose tanker, this one. Wine one week, milk the next. Then they'd have to climb inside to clean it out before it took on petrol, or what have you. Come on, Brenda. Let's get you two back to civilisation. I've got to pick up hamburgers for the crew."

There were cheers as they entered the community hall. Nils was embraced by a small blonde who hugged him with passionate relief. He kissed his wife eagerly.

The controller came across to her. "I've bad news for you, I'm afraid. You live on Paradine Avenue, don't you?"

Brenda nodded. Her mouth was too dry to speak.

"It's all gone," the man said. "We lost every house along that stretch. We got everyone out in time, except one pig-headed bugger who stayed on his roof hosing it down until the power went off."

"That would be my Mirek," Brenda croaked.

"Oh. That explains it. He got the garden hose and went back up but the pressure was right down, what with us drawing so much from the mains. Here, Ainsley, tell Brenda about her house. You were on that crew, weren't you?"

"Sure was. Sorry about your bad luck, Mrs Bodanovic. Your man just stood there, watching the house burn, until we heard this terrible scream from inside. He just yelled, "Hell. I forgot Roger!" and ran into the flames before we could stop him. Then this thing flew out, all aflame. We hosed it down but it was too late. It keeled over and died. Your man's clothes were burnt to a cinder and his hair was alight."

"Mirek's dead?" Brenda felt like fainting.

"No, he'll live. He's just getting his burns dressed. That's him, now."

Brenda turned and saw the bent and blackened figure limping painfully towards her, arms open in love.

"I'm sorry, I'm sorry," he cried. "I let you down. I couldn't save the house. I couldn't even save the bloody parrot. I thought I was going to die and all I could think about was how much I love you and how much I'd let you down."

Great howls of anguish burst from Brenda's throat. She was speechless, tortured, guilt-ridden. Her soul felt as if it was curling at the edges, shrivelling like burning paper.

"Don't. Don't," Mirek said. "Don't cry, Brenda. There's nothing lost that can't be replaced.

But there was, there was, and her heart knew it. So she just sobbed helplessly and clung more tightly to the man she had betrayed.

"We can rebuild," he said, stroking her hair. "We can start all over again."

"But not here," she cried. "Not here. Back in the city, Mirek."

She stared across the hall and met the eye of Nils. He winked and Brenda shut her mind.

She never wanted to see that look again.

Hey-ho, The Daddy-o

"Why have you decided to emigrate to Australia?" asked the journalist, conducting an interview for High Fliers International, a television program for CNC. "You're at the height of your career. You've not only broken through the glass ceiling but you're obviously dancing on the roof."

"I'm going to be married," Cerise Farraday replied, fending off further questions about the lucky man. She knew quite well the drawback to glass ceilings was that those underneath could see up her skirt, but it was a fact of life and, being who and what she was, she was determined they would pay handsomely for the privilege. They did. They begged her to reveal everything. She was the most exciting motivational speaker and organisational guru any of them had met.

"I've been very lucky in my business life. Now it's time to move to the next phase of my life plan." She looked at her watch pointedly.

The journalist reminded viewers that Cerise had been awarded the title of Britain's Miss Fixit, Business Woman of the Decade. "I thought you didn't believe in luck," he said.

Cerise laughed. "Luck is something you make, not something which hits you like blind fate. I got to the top through clever planning and hard work."

"You were offered scholarships to both Oxford and the London School of Economics, but you left school at seventeen to take a cadetship in industry, studied business administration at night school, took an external degree while running various departments with a ruthless efficiency, and were assistant general manager of International Business Systems by the time you were twenty-four. Is that correct?"

"Yes. I matriculated early and found school boring. I couldn't see myself locked in lecture theatres for years. I wanted to get my teeth into life and tear me off a chunk."

"Offered the plum job at IBS, you resigned to start Troubleshooters Inc.'

"I did. By then I was speaking on transactional analysis, internal structures, the paperless office, personnel without pain, flow-warp accounting, cash cows and how to milk them, planning, policies and politics."

The journalist consulted his notes. "I believe that failing companies sought your services and you pulled them out of the red, fledgling entrepreneurs sought advice and you showed them how to fly, Government departments contracted you to dig them out of the mire. You added international negotiating to your repertoire, became a jet-setter with briefcase, one of Europe's Best Dressed Ten and a millionaire by the time you were thirty. Have you had any time for a personal life?"

"Yes, of course, but it's structured." There was always a personable escort on hand, often a celebrity, though she could claim to be that in her own right. There were operas and the races, first nights and fine dining. She was seen in the right places with the right people, which was good business networking.

"Have you had time for romance? Have you time for a sex life?"

" Mind your own business!" she snapped. Was there no limit to the intrusive nature of interviewers? She was beginning to feel sorry she had agreed to this one.

"What motivated you to choose Australia for your new home, Miss Farraday?"

"The Olympic Games. Sydney 2000 was so devastatingly well organised, its opening ceremony showing such flair, such imagination, such precision, that I felt I could live there with confidence because Australia does not seem to need my particular skills. I want to be able to concentrate on marriage and motherhood, on agriculture and life on the land. Britain was making unreasonable demands on my time and energy."

"You've been described as having the potential of another Mrs Thatcher. Political analysts say you could to cut drainage channels through the quagmire of tradition which is swamping progress. Is it true that a safe seat and the Ministry of Industry and Energy has been offered to you?"

"Oh, quite true, but it does not fit in with my life plan. I told you, I'm getting married. I made a plan when I was sixteen and I have never deviated from it." She got up, signifying that the interview was over. She had maintained her poise and kept her thoughts to herself.

Her biological clock was bleeping. Her plan showed that, having achieved all previous goals, it was time to marry and have two children, scientifically conceived to ensure a boy then a girl, genetically tested and properly nurtured with folic acid, and taught to love music at the foetal stage. She craved sunshine, minimal pollution, and a challenge. The Winter Olympics had clinched her resolve. The ice skater (what was his name?) who won gold by staying on his feet when everyone else had tumbled in a heap, was the sort of man she needed. Not the fastest, but a stayer, one with a streak of luck and a cheerful optimism.

After all, as she well knew, luck was not haphazard, it was made. Given relatively unpromising material she, and she alone, could turn a man into a medal winner. She was relieved the interviewer had not persisted with questions about her intended. She would have felt foolish admitting that, as yet, she had no idea who he was to be.

"The farmer wants a wife!" The headline, drawn from an

irritating children's game, had caught the eye of Cerise as she flicked through magazines at Australia House. There was a three page spread of young, bronzed Anzacs, sprinkled with the more mature sort, all country men who were finding it hard to find women because the ladies could do better for themselves in the cities.

"Yes!" said Cerise, reading it. "Yes, yes, yes!"

She decided, while looking at the specimens in the magazine, that a farmer - or rather, a pastoralist and grazier, a cocky...a quaint antipodean phrase...would suit her purposes. She slipped the magazine into her briefcase, dazzled the interview team with her qualifications, her charm and her illusionary good looks, and waved her bank balance in front of them. There was no doubt she qualified for business migration. They promised her papers would be fast-tracked.

In the interim she hired an investigator to look more closely at the backgrounds of the hunks whose brief description and physical appearance most appealed to her. It was not encouraging. One had run through a large field of applicants and seemed more likely to start a harem than settle down, three had got hitched to the first woman who was half-way passable, the oldest prospect had halitosis and two had fallen in love with one another and were living in bliss at Surfers Paradise.

Of the others, only one replied to her letter. Glyn Dower, a sixth-generation mixed farmer, from Rhondda Bend, said he'd be happy to consider a Pom as his parents had been very much attached to the old country. In fact, he wrote, they'd gone back to Wales every year to attend the Eisteddfod at Llangollen.

"Very cultural, they were," he said. "Very into the history. Loved the music. Mam had a thing about Tom Jones. Do you look like Charlotte Church?"

Cerise looked at his photograph. Not exactly the bronzed

Anzac model. Yes, you could see the rugged Taff in Glyn. He had broken his nose playing rugby. He had the same kind of battered good looks Richard Burton had worn, and look where those had got him. Into Elizabeth Taylor. Twice. And onto the bottle. However, there was nothing in the report to suggest Glyn was an alcoholic. Moreover, on the level of income he was earning from Rhondda Bend, it was hard to see how he could afford a habit of that nature.

"I could cope with a social drinker," Cerise told the investigator. "After all, have the businessmen in London have pickled their livers by the time they're forty."

She rang Glyn. He had a voice like Burton, deep and rounded, his tongue mellifluous but overlain with strong Australian vernacular.

"Come and stay on the farm," he suggested. "Sort of have a trial, isn't it? See if I'm the sort of bloke whose bed you could put your slippers under."

"And if I'm the sort of sheila...it is sheila you call girls, isn't it?..that you could look at over the breakfast table every morning."

"You don't wear curlers, do you? I wouldn't fancy a bird with curlers."

Cerise, whose hair was cut by the stylist who once looked after Princess Di, assured him she was not that way inclined.

"Good-oh. Make sure you pack your welly-boots, won't you?"

*

After months of interesting letters, in which a tentative understanding had been reached, Glyn Dower failed to meet Cerise when she landed at Perth International. She piled her crocodile-skin luggage on a trolley and waited impatiently for his arrival. When her name was called on the PA system she went to the customer service counter.

"Mr Dower rang to say he's been unable to get away from the property as he's had trouble with Hughie," the ground hostess said. "He suggests you take the train to Bunbury and he'll meet you at Brunswick Junction."

Cerise was not amused. So much for Australian sunshine. There was an icy wind. She was shivering by the time the taxi got to Perth Central station. There were no porters. Train was not her chosen mode of travel. There was no first class carriage. A nun, accompanied by two snotty-nosed children, sat on the vacant seat opposite her. The nun told her rosary and didn't tell off the children, who ran up and down the aisle. They ate sweets and wiped their sticky fingers on her luggage. Armadale, Byford, Mundijong, North Dandalup. The annoyances got out at Pinjarra. Waroona, Yarloop, Harvey, Cookernup. Two hours of similar landscapes, a range of hills to the east, flat, grassy plains to the west. All the same.

Fields full of cows. She corrected herself. Paddocks full of cows. Cerise had studied ruminants. She had taken a crash course in farming in the time since her interview and her marital inspiration. She was a speed reader with a retentive memory.

Brunswick Junction next stop. Cerise sighed with relief. She straightened the seams on her stockings, all the rage that year, and combed her hair. A lick of lip gloss, a dab of powder, a slurp of Poison. She inched her cases close to the carriage door and waited eagerly for the train to slide into the station.

Glyn Dower was the only person on the platform. He was all over her like an untrained puppy. She felt like saying, "Sit! Stay! Down boy!"

"G'day," said Glyn, plonking her a hearty kiss. He smelled good, of Brut. He hefted her cases, tucking the travel bags under long arms which would have looked proportionate on a gorilla. He had no trouble in carrying all four pieces at once.

"At least he's strong," Cerise thought. "A little shorter than I expected and rather hairy, but that's a sign of virility, they say."

"Sorry about not meeting you but Hughie really let me down. Had to get the cattle into shelter on me own. Can't rely on anything these days. Hughie never thinks about us poor farming blokes. Got snow on the Stirling Range, but what do we want with snow at this time of year? You cold, or what? Got me a thick blanket in the station wagon. You'd better wrap yourself in it. Your arms are blue."

"Hasn't this car got a heater?" asked Cerise.

"Hasn't worked since the last trouble we had with Hughie." Glyn was too embarrassed to admit that he'd driven the car into the creek last time there'd been a bit of a flood on the Rhondda River. He'd been washed off the bitumen and had buggered the electrics.

He cut through the back roads heading for Collie. "We're out past the coalmines, near Cardiff," he said. "Little spread near Bowelsup. That's us." He handed her the map. "Rhondda Bend, out of Bowelsup, near Cardiff. Reminded the Dowers of the old country."

"Bowelsup?" Cerise spluttered, looking at the spelling. How could she tell friends she was living near a place spelt Bowelsup, no matter how it was pronounced.

Her visions of classic pastoralists and graziers faded. Glyn was not even cut from the cocky cloth. By his looks he could barely be what she classed as farmer. Country bumpkin sprang to mind though he was not at all uncouth. Very much the gentleman, in fact.

Rhondda Bend was more substantial than she expected on

meeting its owner. He parked the car on the top of the hill and pointed down to a wide valley with a silver stream among the trees at the bottom.

"I own all this," Glyn said modestly, waving his hand upstream and down. "Good grazing land down under and nice arable paddocks on the top. Mixed crops. Apples on the other side of the valley. Sell them to a juice factory. Sorry we had to come the long way round but Hughie's buggered the road through the valley."

The farmhouse was out of sight until they crested a fold in the hill and drove past an isolated church.

"Mam and Dad are buried there," said Glyn. "I planted daffodils on Mam's grave and leeks on Dad's. Close enough so I can walk up in the evening and have a yarn with them about old times."

Cerise felt sorry for him. Fancy having only the dead for company. "Don't you get out to meet people?" she asked.

"I sure do. I play rugby for Bowelsup at the weekend and go over to Cardiff for darts on a Tuesday. They're a good bunch of blokes. Every week I go, Hughie permitting."

The farmhouse was close to the valley floor. It looked unkempt, the garden a wreck, the verandahs sagging. There was a henhouse, canted on its side in the bottom of the home paddock. The hens were on the loose. Cerise stepped in some poop as she got out of the car.

"Sorry about that," Glyn said, wiping her shoe with a ragged handkerchief which he shoved back in his pocket. "I haven't had time to fix the chook pens since Hughie pushed them over."

Picking her way through the droppings, Cerise climbed the steps to the building, which was set on stumps, leaving a space below the floor.

"Handy for the dog," said Glyn. "Slept under there."

"You haven't got a dog, have you?"

"Went swimming last time Hughie came through. He won't be back. We'll get another. Here's your room. I turned the electric blanket on. You want a shower or something? I've got a casserole in the oven."

Clean, well-fed, for Glyn could cook superbly, Cerise felt exhaustion overtake her. She made excuses and said she'd go to bed.

"I expect I'll sleep the clock round," she yawned. "I can't sleep on aeroplanes."

"Then you'll not mind if I go to Cardiff to play darts, will you?"

She shrugged. "Just don't wake me when you come in."

Glyn didn't. In fact, when she woke up the next morning, there was no sign that he'd come in at all. She dressed warmly, put on her welly-boots, and decided to explore. She walked down to the creek and found Glyn's car, upside down in the bed of the small river. He'd run off the road and had been hanging in his seat belt all night.

"Get an ambulance," he groaned. "I've broken my leg."

Two hours later he was on his way to Bunbury Hospital, suffering from hypothermia, an unusual occurrence in an Australian summer. Cerise followed the ambulance in Glyn's car. She was relieved to find Bunbury was a modern city, small, but of considerable charm.

"You won't run out on me, will you?" Glyn pleaded, as the nurse prepared him for surgery. "You'll stay and look after the farm? I could be in here for weeks, in traction."

"What should I do?"

"Hey, if you are serious about being the next Mrs Dower, you can do whatever you like," he said. "You are going to marry me, aren't you?"

"Do you want me to?"

He smiled. "I think I need you," he said. "You're pretty. You'll do me."

Cerise's heart turned over at that smile. It was very attractive. He was right. He did need her. He needed her like crazy. So she smiled back. He asked her to pass him his jacket. There was a jeweller's box in it, containing an engagement ring with a large emerald.

"It's not real," he said. "But it's all I could afford. That's why I wrote and asked what colour your eyes were."

"You really are a romantic, aren't you?" said the bride-to-be, making no protest when he slid the ring onto her finger. It didn't fit, but she could have that fixed at the same time she replaced the stone with a genuine one. He need never know.

Cerise went straight from the hospital to the bank. She opened an account and presented her references. The manager rang for sherry. It was, he said, a pity about the bad luck of the Dowers. The floods had swept right down the Rhondda valley, through the homestead, washing away the chooks and the cattle on the water meadows.

"Happened almost every year," he said. "I told old Owen the climate was changing and this part of the south-west was in for wetter seasons while the north of the state was getting drier, but he wouldn't have it. His wife said it didn't matter. She'd never wanted carpets and she just hosed the place out when the water level dropped. Said it was like spring cleaning. But it killed her in the end. He drowned trying to save the dog and she caught double pneumonia."

"It won't happen again," Cerise said firmly. "That's good land. It just needs to be managed properly."

She charmed her way into the office of the man from the regional Agriculture Department. They had a deep and meaningful. She dropped in at the local shire council on her way back to the farm. The executives agreed that something should be done.

Cerise, having drawn up short and long term goals, got someone in to milk the cows, left the chooks to their own devices, and flew to Perth. If dirty money greases many palms, clean money is more effective. Cerise delivered metaphoric castor oil to political parties, had high-level discussions and unstopped the blockages of bureaucracy.

The local council agreed to the first phase. There was, they said, no reason why she should not relocate the house, provided an environmentally-friendly septic system was installed. Within the week the earth-moving contractors had leveled and compacted a new site on the shoulder of the valley, just below the church. A building surveyor had pronounced the homestead solid, though in need of restumping as there was rot in the supports.

The future Mrs Dower said, "No way! I'm having a good concrete foundation with a damp course."

And it was so. The stumping contractors were quick and precise. The plumbers connected the septics and revamped the bathroom with a modern spa, the electricians rewired the whole house while installing reverse cycle air-conditioning. Old floorboards were replaced with slate in the kitchen and parquet in the formal areas, while good wool carpets went down in the bedrooms.

Cerise stayed in the hotel in Cardiff while the work was in progress. She talked sheep with sheep farmers, cattle with dairymen, chooks with poulterers and grapes with vintners. She also learned how to play darts and bought herself life membership of the Bowelsup rugby club. She drove to Bunbury twice a week to see Glyn and didn't say a word about the changes she was making. She talked darts and rugby, for this was the sort of news he enjoyed.

He was pleased she was making an effort to fit into the community. He was glad to confound the predictions of his mates who said marrying an older woman wouldn't do and had urged him to send for a Russian bride.

"You little ripper," he said, stroking her arm. "You scored a double top?" This woman had style. She was a good-looker too, stacked where it counted. Lying in bed for weeks had not cooled his ardour. He was eager to get out of plaster and test drive Cerise.

That would have to wait, said the orthopaedics man. There were complications. The bone was not healing and metal plates had to be inserted. It could be months, he warned. Glyn worried about Cerise, all alone and the farm going to rack and ruin.

"I got the hay in," she said.

"The bailer is stuffed. How did you manage that?"

"It was only the gridder flange on the frangleburter," she replied. "I just tightened it up and gave it a good oil."

His jaw dropped. "How did you learn to do that?"

"Didn't I tell you I did mechanics at school? I like fiddling with engines." She didn't tell him one of her few physical hobbies was driving sports cars at Brands Hatch. She could read manuals as well as the next man. "By the way, Glyn, would you mind if I built a fish pond?"

"Build what you like, darling. Anything to make you happy."

It had been a bit of a battle to get approval from Water and

Rivers but in the end they let her dam the Rhondda. The council and Main Roads were happy when she offered to stand the cost of building a bridge over the creek, since they had not got round to repairing the damaged road, which would end up under two metres of water. The council even agreed to construct a car park on the far bank to service the new trout farm. When the water settled, the shire president came to the small function at which the fingerlings were poured into their new home.

"You could use some marron in there," he said.

This was a new one on Cerise. Freshwater crayfish had not crossed her mind. She smiled sweetly. "I count on you to advise me," she said. "How soon can I start building the trout farm offices and shop? And is it worth considering a restaurant next to it?"

"Only if my daughter can have the lease," he said, grinning. "She's a fine chef!"

By the time Glyn was ready for discharge the top arable land had been put down to vines. As the water meadows had been flooded, the future Mrs Dower had taken Rhondda Bend out of milk production in favour of raising quality beef. The cows had been inseminated by Malloway Greatorex III, who'd won prizes at the Royal Show.

It was time, she felt, that she had similar treatment from Glyn Dower. She suggested they marry in Bunbury and spend a few days on honeymoon at the Lord Forrest Hotel. Glyn, she was glad to find out, was as great a champion as the prize bull and, since she studied marital arts with the same attention to detail as she gave to everything else in her life, he was surprised at her versatility, given that he'd discovered her to be a virgin. Cerise, who had regarded the whole process as an intellectual exercise, was delighted to find it enjoyable.

It was in a state of total exhaustion and mutual admiration

that they returned to Rhondda Bend. The lakes were limpid under the gum trees along the creek. Glyn thought Cerise, who was driving, must have taken a wrong turning for he did not recall this stretch of country. He did not recognise the farmhouse near the church, for it had been painted white and the grounds had been landscaped. Nor did he know anyone round Cardiff grew grapes, but row after row of baby vines made a distinctive pattern on the landscape.

"Welcome home, darling," she cooed. "I've bought you a wedding present."

Glyn, pinching himself, sat down gingerly on his mother's favourite rocking chair outside the front door, which was one thing he recalled from the old days. Even that had been repolished and given a new chintz cushion. Cerise came out of the house carrying a small puppy, which she placed on Glyn's lap. It had been delivered that morning by one of Glyn's mates, Hughie, who bred kelpies. He'd left it in the outside laundry.

"Hughie tells me he's house-trained," she said. The puppy immediately relieved himself on on Glyn's trousers.

It was, after all, no surprise, thought Cerise. Any man named after the pagan god, Hugh the Lu, worshipped by Cornish miners and Welsh rugby players with equal devotion, and blamed for any act of unforeseen weather, could not be expected to be reliable.

She decided to name the pup after its breeder. It seemed as if it was going to piddle all over the place. "Naughty Hughie," she said. "Bad dog!"

*

Eight years later Cerise watched as Glyn backed the new PeopleMover out of the garage. They needed a large vehicle. Glyn had proven not only very virile but to carry a genetic predisposition to twins. They had two boys first and two girls followed. Then, just to prove every plan does not go according to schedule, they had a pigeon pair. Cerise did not leave it to chance after that. Menopause might be round the corner but, with Glyn's insatiable appetite for hey-ho the daddy-o she felt it was wise to have her tubes tied. Hormone replacement therapy would take care of the change of life but breeding like a rabbit would seriously throw her plans out of kilter.

Luckily...by good foresight and motivational guidance in the right direction...Glyn was a superb house-husband. He left farming to her. He cooked like a dream. She ran the businesses. He was president of the Bowelsup rugby club and captain of the darts' team. She was a leading figure in country politics. Once the youngest were at school she accepted the offer of a safe seat and was now Minister for Agriculture and Industry. Before taking the children to school Glyn would drop her at the landing strip at the top of the hill, where a light aircraft would pick her up for the trip to Parliament.

She listened as the children danced around, singing, "The farmer wants a wife, the farmer wants a wife, hey-ho the daddy-o, the farmer wants a wife." It was all going according to plan.

Hughie, now a fat and contented kelpie, waddled over to her and cocked his leg against the red box with the Cabinet papers. He was still an inveterate dribbler. A shadow crossed the grass. There was a small, dark cloud overhead. It looked as if it was going to bucket right over Rhondda Bend. Hugh the Lu was about to dump on her.

Cerise, who'd had serious thoughts about global weather control, glared at it."You wouldn't bloody dare," she snapped, having learned the most common epithet in Australia. "I warn you, Hughie!"

And Hugh the Lu, lurking in the cloud, knowing luck was made, not fated, decided not to risk upsetting the future Prime

Minister of Australia. He evaporated.

According To Darwin

Queensland Lion Dogs are all the rage this year. You've seen them. Russell Crowe has one and so has Kylie Minogue. Oprah Winfrey has two. We gave her one and she bought a second, a male. If she thinks she's got a breeding pair, we've got news for her. We sterilise all lion dogs before sale so would-be owners have to come to us for their pets. This means we can control the purity of the bloodline and, by ensuring the breed is rare, keep the price up to the exorbitant levels we now enjoy. You haven't seen a lion dog? Where have you been? In the backwoods? I'm only joking because the backwoods is where lion dogs were developed. Let me describe one to you. The face is long and elegant, the muzzle aristocratic, the ears finely pricked and upstanding. They are similar in size to a greyhound, but a little larger, breeding being what it is, selective of the best stock. They have long, silky golden hair rippling down to knee height. This is stiffer around the neck, and forms a ruff like a lion's mane, hence the name of the breed. They are beautiful animals, affectionate and loyal, easily trained and, joy oh joy, do not moult their coats. They enjoy and need grooming, however, and one of the reasons we are so protective of the species is to ensure they are sold only to those certain to give them their regular supplements, for we supply enough extract to last a lifetime.

Giving a few away to celebrities soon established the demand and now our order books are full, even at $3500 a head. Last year we kept four more breeding pairs so, with each pair producing a litter of at least eight, we should have an income of about $300,000 a year. Of course, not all breed true to type. There's a recessive gene in there, which makes about twenty per cent resistant to the growth of long hair. The top pelt doesn't come in until the fourth month after birth and at the nine-month stage I cull them. My grandfather used to return the throwbacks to the islands off Arnhemland and let them take their chances in the wild but I thought it a crime to waste good protein. I got a permit to kill them for meat. I freeze the carcasses and tan the skins and, once a year, a trader from Cambodia brings a freezer truck up from Brisbane and exports the lot back home, because dog meat is a delicacy in his country.

Even so, the income from the sideline doesn't allow us a prosperous life style, here on the border of New South Wales and Queensland. Still, Kiri and I reckon my parents were lucky to find this property; tucked in behind the ranges south of the Cunningham Gap, off that God-awful dirt road which runs on the top of the ridge ten clicks east of the New England Highway. You'd never know we were there, for we get no mail delivery except to a Post Office box in Toowoomba. We don't complain because so far the local authorities either side of the border seem to think we belong to the other mob and neither sends us rate notices or demands for land tax. We've got our own well and a generator, we can't get normal television but can run DVDs off the satellite-linked computers, which no longer rely on telegraph lines. We did without until technology caught up with our needs because telegraph poles would be a dead give-away that we're here, and we like the solitude. We even have a dead tree across the gate from the road, making it look as if the track is never used. We shop in Warwick, Toowoomba, Ipswich, or Tenterfield, never the same place twice running, and we join no churches, no clubs. We like animals better than people.

School? Goodness me, no. My wife, Kiri, refused to drive to Legume every day and insisted on education by correspondence for our boy. We thought of boarding school but, frankly, couldn't afford it while trying to live as self-sufficiently as possible. When the last of our savings were gone we had to go into business, breeding the dogs to sell. It was Kiri's inspiration. I never would have thought of turning my hobby into a paying concern. It was Mum who thought up the name, Queensland Lion Dogs, and she who suggested we get a web-site rather than have mail come to the property's PO Box, as the longer we remained a mystery to the tax-man, the better.

Once a year, after the annual sales, Dad and I leave Kiri and Mum in charge and sail off on the Huon Venturer, the old wooden schooner which belonged to great-great-grandfather, who sailed to Pukka Pukka in 1901. He got so angry about Federation, and plans to log his corner of the world, that he packed his wife, kid, dogs, cats, goats and chickens onto his boat and sailed to find somewhere he and he alone could rule the roost. He had two sets of encyclopaedias and that was all the schooling he or his child would need, he said.

Don't look for Pukka Pukka on the maps. It's not there. It's somewhere off the shipping routes, east of the Tasman Sea, and that's all I'm saying. The island is the top of a volcanic mountain, lush with forest, with a crater lake in the centre around which great pines tower. There was enough flat land for a farm and good timber for building. The stock flourished, especially the dogs. They developed a taste for a certain type of spurge that grew under the forest canopy. It's a pale green plant with a milky sap, much like a euphorbia. I'd have expected it to be poisonous but they treated it like cat-nip. They also enjoyed chewing on the green mussels that grew thickly on the rocks around the reef enclosing the lagoon.

You've got to remember there had been forty years of debate about Darwin's theory of evolution and my ancestor was as interested in the subject as any, having bred greyhounds in Northern Ireland before being transported. He wanted to know if the new hairiness was simply a variant caused by a change of diet and climate, or a genuine mutation that could be inherited. That's when and why he started breeding to enhance their characteristics.

Two wars passed by our family. Each generation got educated using the encyclopaedias, though some volumes were getting pretty tatty. By the time they came to me, S to U was missing, which was why I had trouble identifying the particular spurge involved. Knew little about singers and sewing, telephones, tigers, umbrellas and unicorns, turkeys and turnips either. My boy complained about the lack of C to E so I picked up a newer Britannica at a second-hand bookshop last April. I might read S to U next winter.

A couple of times a year Dad and I would take Mum on the schooner to New Zealand, stocking up with supplies on marathon shopping trips. That's where I met Kiri, my wife by arrangement. We sold rare purple paua shell and jade, which was quarried from the centre of the island. This income allowed us to maintain our independence. Only when France decided to carry out atomic tests at Mururoa Atoll did father decide Pukka Pukka was not too safe any more. He did a lucrative deal with Jack the Rat and started hunting for a hideaway in Australia. That was how we came by our own piece of paradise but the compensation money ran out five years ago.

For a decade Dad and I made the annual voyage to harvest the spurge and convert it into an extract, which is later added to mussel oil and formed into capsules for the lion dogs. We've tried to grow it from seed but there's something in the soil at Pukka Pukka which is unique. I'm trying desperately to find a biochemical company that will make a synthetic version, for there have been strange rumblings on the island and there is a cone of ash in one comer of the crater lake. There are sulphurous bubblings around the shore and a great gash has opened in the side of the lagoon, making access through the reef easier, although it means sharks can now get into those peaceful waters more easily. My wife, whose family are Maori and fish those waters regularly, reported a massive eruption in March and a pillar of fire rising on the horizon on the bearings where Pukka Pukka lay.

I was so worried I wrote to the Western Plains Zoo at Dubbo and asked if they could identify the spurge and could suggest any similar species that might be conducive to hairiness. A boffin wrote to say that, if there was, he'd be selling it to men with bald heads. However, he was driving up to Brisbane for a conference and would drop in and talk to me..

He admired the lion dogs very much but confessed he'd never be able to afford one. I showed him the breeding records going back for nearly sixty years. I took him out to the greenhouses to look at the spurge we had managed to propagate. I showed him the silos full of dried spurge and the tanks of mussel oil

"When that runs out, the lion dogs will revert to their original form, I suspect," I said. "It's a recessive gene, I feel sure. Without the golden pelt they're ugly-looking dogs; too much of the greyhound in them, all lean and slinky around the hindquarters."

I took him down to the breeding pens to show him the six-month-old pups, glorious little bundles of fluff with bright-eyes. I loved to watch them playfully tumbling around the yard. He lit his pipe and leaned on the rails, looking thoughtful

"What are the variants like?" asked the boffin. "I'd like to see them."

"We keep them down there, isolated. I fatten them up for market before culling. Ugly little sods, aren't they? Striped like runty zebras."

The boffin was purple-red in the face and spluttering. "You blithering eff-wit!" he gasped. "Worrying yourself sick about your effing lion dogs? Don't you know what a breeding pair of Tasmanian Tigers would be worth?"

Typical of boffins. You ask them one question and, if they don't have an easy answer, they change the subject. Well, two can play at that game.

I had to drag him away from the culling pens down to the chook yard. "'I thought you might like to see my South Pacific turkeys," I said. "I don't know what to do with them. They breed like mad but they're too big for the average oven."

I hadn't noticed the man had a speech defect before. His eyes bulged and he grunted, "Doh-doh-doh-doh!" Presume he was going to say don't do something but he never got to tell us. He waved his arms around and then passed out.

Dad helped me lift him into his four-wheel-drive and followed as I took him to hospital in Toowoomba. It was, the doctors said, a massive stroke. He might not recover.

"Blown his mind, the doctor said," Dad remarked, putting our jeep into gear.

"Not much of a mind to blow, was there, not knowing the difference between a lion and a tiger!" I replied. "We all know tigers come from India. Did you see his face when he saw the turkeys?"

Dad grinned. "Reckon he was missing S to U and all. Bit of a dog, that bloke."

Double Trouble

Bridie MacGuire was right-hand, left-hand challenged. She had always been clumsy, of course, and therefore took great care over what she did in order to avoid making mistakes. There was nothing she hated more than to bawled out over something trivial, unless it was being mocked at for stupidity. She was a big, shy, plain girl who, under the spotlight of other people's anger, felt herself shrivelling until she was just a sweaty grease-spot on the stage of life.

She wasn't stupid; far from it. She'd sailed through her nursing degree and graduated with honours. Some said she should have been studying medicine, but Bridie didn't have the confidence to push herself forward.

"I like helping people who are sick," she told her father. "And I just love working with children. I couldn't have gone through all the stress of being an intern, rushing here and there, making snap decisions, facing emergencies, trying to think of a hundred things at once. No, I'm happy where I am, in the Children's Hospital."

"It seems such a waste of a good brain," her father said. "If you change your mind and want to become a doctor, I'll foot the bill."

"You're one in a million, Dad. Just let me be. It suits me, being slow and careful and having time to love the little darlings."

That was Bridie, careful and kind. It made her an exceptional nurse, especially of difficult children.

The right-hand, left-hand problem was not obvious until her parents bought her a car. Her instructor nearly went crazy teaching her to drive for, when he said right, she turned left. When he said, "Left hand down a bit," she jerked the wheel to the right. Reversing lessons were a nightmare. She got a licence only by taking the utmost care.

Having the freedom of the road gave her no sense of elation. She recognised the weakness had contributed to her clumsiness in the past. Being Bridie, she built into her routines a deliberate double check on left and right. She made a point of asking those who said, "Take the bottle on the right," whether they meant on the speaker's right or on the hearer's right. One of the surgeons noted it and dubbed her "Get It Right MacGuire." Claude Trumbill was an irascible pig of a man whose operations were a scene of oaths and high drama, who never took the blame for mistakes and who, eventually, told the Theatre Sister to get rid of the MacGuire girl before he killed her.

Her colleagues thought it amusing. They hated working with Trumbill and felt Bridie had been clever to have got out of her stint of theatre so quickly.

"You may laugh, but better safe than sorry," said Bridie. "That's why I always check what medicines the doctors have ordered. You'll not catch me giving an overdose by mistake!"

"But what do you do if you think an error has been made?" said a colleague. "I wouldn't dare question what a doctor has said."

"I would," said Bridie, who secretly dreaded the possibility of having to do so. "After all, what's the worst they can do to you? Bellow and bawl? They can't sack you for asking questions."

"No, but they can sack you for being right! It's what's called a cover-up, Bridie MacGuire."

"Phooey!" said Bridie. "Check and double check. We've got a union, haven't we? And there's always the power of the press!"

"You wouldn't!"

Bridie drew a deep breath and examined her conscience. "I

would, if circumstances demanded it," she muttered.

Little did she know the power of the press was about to descend on her in an unexpected manner. An international humanitarian agency, working in Madagascar, had begged medical help for three-year-old Pierre Umdobo. He had a sarcoma on his right leg, a cancer of the bone which, if not treated rapidly, could metastasise through his entire body. Rotary International had raised the fare to send him to Australia, the hospital board had agreed to waive its fees and Sister Angelique had acted as escort, for she was coming home on furlough.

Claude Trumbill, who headed the oncology unit, was not impressed. He did not like giving freebies. He had just returned from a conference at the Mayo Clinic and was about to fly to New Delhi, where he was to be a keynote speaker on Post-operative Prosthetics. He was a partner in a company which made artificial limbs. Time was pressing. However, he knew a good public relations exercise when he saw one. He was photographed holding little Pierre and, at his press conference, extracts of which went on the news, pledged on-going support for the child.

"As you know, I sail my ocean-going yacht to South Africa every year to enjoy a safari. I will make an annual detour to Madagascar with a new prosthesis for little Pierre until he stops growing."

"That means amputation?" asked a Channel Seven mouthpiece.

"It's the standard treatment for sarcoma," said the great man.

Bridie was furious. She had been delegated to special Pierre Umdobo because she spoke French. It was she who had to break the news to Sister Angelique.

"Oh dear," said the nun. "We hoped so much that medical

research in Australia was more advanced than in Tananarive. We could have amputated there, but what sort of a life will the child have with only one leg in a tropical country? It is virtually condemning him to a life as a beggar. Maybe I should have taken him to Paris but his father is poor, a school-teacher, and the mother died last year in child-birth. It seemed only sensible to take Pierre and his brother Philippe with me when I came home, in the hope that there could be a bone marrow transplant."

So Bridie did what she had always said she'd do if she thought a mistake was being made. When she took Pierre from Claude Trumbill's arms she said, "I don't think you should cut his leg off!"

The surgeon turned on her angrily. "Oh, so you don't, Nurse Get it Right MacGuire? What would you do?"

"I'd tissue type and run a magnetic resonance imaging scan to see how far the tumour has penetrated. Then I'd think about chemo and radio-therapy and try a transplant."

The man looked as if he would explode. He made noises like a turkey-cock, gobble-gobble-gobble. "You silly little girl! What do you think this tumour is going to be doing while you chase a compatible donor? Twiddling its fingers? No. It's going to be spreading throughout the child's body, into his lymph glands, into his liver, into his brain. That leg should have come off a month ago. Get out of my sight, MacGuire. Get it right! Go roll a bandage!"

"But...but...but," said Bridie, to the great man's back.

Pierre had started to cry when the surgeon shouted. Bridie felt like doing so too, but the child stopped when reunited with his brother. They were as like as peas in a pod. Their skin was a rich chocolate brown, their heads were covered in tight, tufted curls and they ran a fine line in cheeky smiles. She loved them to death. They were all kisses and cuddles. She popped a peppermint in

Philippe's mouth and a banana chewy in Pierre's.

They had quite different tastes in food. Philippe had been unable to attend the press conference because he had made himself sick by eating the entire contents of a tube of mint-flavoured toothpaste. Pierre refused to have anything to do with such dental niceties until Sister Angelique produced a tube of Punch and Judy with a fruit flavour. Philippe liked oranges, Pierre preferred bananas and pineapple. Philippe ate meat, Pierre grabbed his brother's vegetables.

It went further than that, Sister Angelique warned. Philippe did not like to wear red, Pierre disliked blue. "Put them both in yellow or white pyjamas," she advised. "They are a tricky little pair of imps. If you rely on colour to tell who is who, they are likely to switch clothes for sheer devilment."

"Is there no certain way to tell them apart?" Bridie was worried.

"Put armbands on them and make sure they don't exchange them. They are capable of anything. And don't expect them to tell you their right names. As cute as a bag of monkeys, the twins are."

Surgery could not be scheduled for another six days. The twins spent the time wrapping themselves around Bridie's heart, taking delight in teasing her by climbing into one another's beds and pretending to be the other. Bridie kept track with a pocket full of lollies. They had not caught on to her subterfuge with peppermints.

Dr Jim Keith, the new oncology registrar, cornered her one evening and begged a coffee. "You were brave, taking on old Tumbril...that's what we call him. Cart the patients down and use the guillotine. But he's right, Bridie. It might take months to get a tissue match and do what you suggested."

"But it wouldn't," she protested. "That was the whole point of Sister Angelique bringing both boys. They don't do bone marrow transplants in Tananarive, but there's a damn good chance of a perfect match with the Umdobo twins. They're identical!"

"The hell they are!" said Jim Keith. "Does old Tumbril know this?"

"Of course he doesn't. He hasn't even read the notes. Sarcoma equals amputation. Full stop."

"Hey, Bridie, are they asleep? If I sedate them, will you help me take DNA samples?"

"You'll not get the results in time to stop old sawbones."

"You bet I will," he said. "Even if I have to stay up all night to do them myself!"

Two days later he slunk into the ward with a face as long and gloomy as that of a bloodhound. "The match is perfect, but old Tumbril wouldn't listen to me either. He said he's not wasting taxpayer money and a complicated procedure on a pro bono case."

"He won't admit he's wrong?"

"That's right. He's wrong, we're right, and the operation will take place tomorrow."

"Oh, damn the man," said Bridie, wiping her eyes.

She kept her face cheerful in the morning. She followed orders and shaved Pierre's leg. Then, because he demanded it, she gave Philippe a quick scrape as well. She painted Pierre's limb in stripes of yellow, red and purple antiseptic so that he looked like a big bird. Philippe said it was, "Tres jolie," and insisted on the same decoration.

Knowing that Philippe would play up while his brother was

in theatre, she gave him a pre-op sedative as well, hoping he would sleep through the trauma of separation. She gave them both big kisses and tucked them into their beds. She couldn't bear to be there when the orderlies came for Pierre. Instead she locked herself in the linen cupboard and had a really good cry.

"Pull yourself together, Bridie MacGuire!" she snapped. "What did you swear you'd do if you saw something wrong? You swore you would go to the press! Hurry, hurry, hurry. Pray you're not too late!"

She rushed back to the ward to get her mobile phone from her handbag. Philippe's bed was empty. She kissed the other sleeping twin. His breath smelt of bananas. There was no time to lose. No time for calling the media. She ran down the corridors to the theatre wing. The operation had started. The child's limb had been draped in green cloths and the area of the cut had been marked in red dots. Claude Trumbill had a sharp saw in his hand and his assistant was standing ready to tie off any blood vessels encountered.

Heedless of the need to wear a gown and scrub, she burst into the room. "Stop!" she yelled. "Stop! You've got it wrong!"

The surgeon roared in anger. "Wrong, Get It Right MacGuire? Don't tell me you've prepped the wrong leg!"

"No. You've got the wrong twin!"

"You're an imbecile, Nurse MacGuire. This is Pierre Umdobo. He was in Pierre Umdobo's bed. His tag says Pierre Umdobo. What makes you think it isn't the right boy?"

She looked around for help, in panic, feeling the waves of anger coming at her from all directions, except one. "Dr Keith, Dr Keith," she cried. "Smell the patient's breath. Does it smell of peppermint?"

He drew down his mask and sniffed deeply. "Yes, that's

peppermint. Strong peppermint. Why?"

"Then that is Philippe. Pierre won't touch mints. They've been up to their tricks again!"

"God damn it to hell!" bellowed Claude Trumbill. "Reschedule the operation for tomorrow."

The Theatre Sister glared at the surgeon. "I'll do no such thing," she snapped. "This whole area has been contaminated and there'll be no more operations in this theatre until it is fully sterile again. And all the other theatres are booked solid."

"Hell's teeth, woman, I fly out to India tomorrow night!"

"Then I suggest you hand the case over to Dr Keith."

"Right. Then I wash my hands of the whole thing!" said Trumbill, throwing the electric saw onto the ground.

Bridie MacGuire, her cap all askew, marched across the theatre and picked up Philippe Umdobo. She kissed her tiny charge and carried him back to the ward.

Two weeks later Patrice Umdobo flew in from Tananarive. Bridie paid for his airfare. "Chemotherapy is making Pierre very sick and miserable," she said to Jim Keith, who'd taken her out to dinner. "He needs his father."

"Let's hope his father appreciates what you've done for the twins."

"I'm thankful Patrice is taking Philippe off our hands part of the day. He's being very fretful."

"Have you got into serious trouble over all of this?"

"The Director of Nursing tore strips off me. But when I told her I'd intended to go to the press about the way the entire case was handled, she went very quiet. I think she's decided I saved the hospital from a major law suit. And so I did!"

"I've asked you this before, Bridie, but I'll ask you again. Are you sure you won't marry me?"

"I can't, Jim. I've promised to marry Patrice Umdobo. I am going to Madagascar to be Maman to the twins."

He sighed. "I don't suppose I can convince you I need you more? That Patrice'd be better off with an African wife?"

"But I love the twins. I love children."

"I could give you some. We could make them together."

"Jim, you should marry my sister, Megan. She's very like me and a whole lot prettier."

Jim smiled. "Bridie, you're wrong about not being pretty. You're beautiful from the inside, shining out. Like this diamond ring. Come on, hold out your hand and promise to marry me."

"Are you sure, Jim?"

"I'm certain, but I'd be happier if you gave me your left hand, not your right!"

Bridie blushed.

"I love you, Get It Right MacGuire," said Dr Keith.

Baby Doll

Jemima did not move. She lay sprawled on the driveway, arms and legs flung wide, her skirt rucked around her waist and a thin trickle of something nasty spilling onto the bitumen beneath her.

Under the sparse straggle of blonde curls was an awful depression that ended above the right eye-socket. Her eye was detached and gleamed glassily and blue from the darkness. Nose and jaw had been pushed to one side with a force that had left a gash from ear to ear, running jaggedly through the line of the rosebud mouth.

As Maisie lifted Jemima's shoulders a strange metallic, grating noise came from the victim's stomach. 'Baby wanna wee-wee.' It was the first sentence Jemima had spoken for years.

Maisie's clumsy fingers spread wide with shock. Even the tears that streamed from her small eyes dried up, though her nose didn't. She wiped it on the back of her sleeve and sat back on her heels, staring at Jemima.

"Mummy kiss Baby." Then came a short silence and a groan. "I wanna go bye-byes."

Ironic that the old doll, whose inner record had been inactive so long, should start again when the stuffing had finally been knocked out of her.

Jemima's mummy said nothing. Her talking mechanism had never worked properly...there was too much tongue in that loose-lipped mouth for Maisie to form anything more than half-words. She could, however, bellow, so she did. She was scared and heartbroken. Jemima was the only one who really understood her.

Her father, Tom Burman, took little notice of her. He stood in the ruins of the flowerbed in front of the house. He swore mightily and shook his fist at the Harley-Davidson, which was roaring down the street in a cloud of dust and petrol fumes, the biker and his foxy lady laughing fit to bust.

"You bleedin' heathens," Tom yelled. "Got no bleedin' respect for man nor beast!"

Maisie's mother came out to see what the fuss was about. She stood on the verandah, wiping her hands on a tea-towel, her plain face with the worried expression it had worn ever since the new neighbours moved in. "The Malloys again? What've they done now?"

"Look at the bleedin' petunias, Pat. That pair of hoons cut right across our front and ruined the petunias. Damn it, they've snapped off the frangipani at the base. Oh, Lord. That's the one mother gave me."

"It's a wonder they didn't run over Maisie. What's she hollerin' about? Is she hurt?"

Tom looked behind him. "No, but her dolly's copped it." He knelt down and put his arms around his daughter, who snuffled against his shoulder.

"Jem bwoke," she muttered thickly.

"We'll mend her. You can be the nurse and I'll be the doctor. Right?"

Maisie nodded. She knew all about hospitals. Though only eight-years-old, she was often a patient herself. "Mend, now."

Tom picked up the battered carcass and gathered the shards of china which had cracked off. "Come on, poppet. First we'll have to ask your mother to put a stitch in Jemima's body. She's losing sawdust like nobody's business."

Pat stretched out the doll on the kitchen table, pushing the breakfast dishes to one side. Maisie fetched the sewing box and watched intently as her mother threaded a needle with stout cotton. Then she rummaged in her toy box until she found her nurse's cap with the red cross on the front. Her thumb was in her mouth and she listened intently as her mother rambled on.

"Grandma had this doll when she was a little girl," she said. "Jemima must be seventy years old, I reckon. You don't get dolls with china heads and rag bodies these days, do you, Tom? Can you mend the head?"

"Maybe, if I can find the right stuff. Have we got any china glue?"

"Under the sink, with the light globes. Have you got any sawdust in the shed?"

"I've got shavings. Take that darned talking gismo out before you sew her up. I can't stand that 'Baby wanna wee-wee' nonsense."

Maisie helped pack the curls of pine into the cavity in Jemima's stomach. Her fingers were short and stubby but were very strong. Her mother praised her warmly and Maisie grinned... a lop-sided smile of happiness.

When the last stitch was in place her father became the chief surgeon. "I'll have to have her head off to fix her face, Pat. Can you cut the drawstring around the neck?"

"You'll have sawdust all over again. Don't get it in the glue."

"I won't. You put Jemima's body in a bag until Maisie and I finish this part." He pulled a reading lamp close to the severed head and started gluing the edges of the broken pieces. His fingers were inside the skull, holding it firm as he eased the jigsaw together. It was not a perfect job. The temple and brow were together, but were rather unshapely. The nose was repositioned on the face. "Can't do any more until this lot's set," he said. "You come out and help me put new plants in the border, Maisie. Then we'll have a cup of tea and finish the work, eh?"

"What about the footie?" Pat asked. "You'll miss the match."

"Bugger the match. Some things are more important," Tom said, ruffling Maisie's hair.

Pat watched them go into the garden, hand in hand. He was wonderful with Maisie, considering. He'd been good with the older children, too, and had never grumbled when the late-in-life baby she'd decided to keep had been born with Down Syndrome. He'd found a special well of love for the poor little mite. Maisie's brothers and sisters followed his example. She was precious to them all. Even the neighbours on the small State Housing Commission estate were kind. Nobody had much money. Timber workers were not part of an affluent society but had a generosity of heart.

Life had been peaceful in Forrestville until the bikers moved in next door to the Burmans. Wild parties, loud music, raised voices, coarse language and the revving of engines had turned the situation into a nightmare. The smell of dope was so thick on the night air that Tom and Pat kept the back of the house closed and spent their evenings on the front verandah, Maisie dozing beside them on a camp bed.

The biker's leader, Gruntfuttock Malloy, accused Tom and Pat of spying on them. When the police came round to break up a particularly riotous party, the gang declared war on the neighbours. There was only a picket fence between the back gardens. Bikers peed through the palings onto Tom's tomato plants. They fired little orange pellets from BB guns and tried to hit the dog, an ancient kelpie known as Docker. They threw beer cans over the fence and tossed fast food boxes onto the lawn under the Burmans' washing line. The Malloys fought constantly. He smacked her around. She retaliated in kind.

Tom called the local council. He wrote to the housing authority. He went to the police and found out about restraining orders. When the moll emptied their garbage bin over the fence, Tom went next door and spoke his mind. Gruntfuttock told him to bugger off. The foxy lady laughed.

Maisie, upset, wandered into the back yard. She pressed her face against the fence and stuck her tongue out at the moll. The Malloy woman was plump and pretty, but wore too much make-up and too few clothes.

"Go away, you little monster." The moll yelled and shied a bottle in Maisie's direction. "Bugger off before I smash yer ugly face in!"

"Leave our girl alone," Pat shouted, coming to the back door. "You lay a finger on Maisie and I'll kill you!"

"Piss off, you old bag. You should have drowned the kid at birth!"

That was a few days before Gruntfuttock ran over the garden for the first time.

Tom was still fuming about it over lunch, though it was his favourite shepherd's pie with peas and mashed potatoes. Maisie liked it too, because she could eat it with a spoon without making too much mess.

While Pat washed up, Tom fixed the lower half of Jemima's face, bracing the work with strips of sticky paper on the outside.

"Aw, darn it," he said. "I should have fixed the eye before I glued the jaw. Now I can't reach the parts that make her eyes open and shut."

Pat took a look. "If you can get a loop of crochet cotton round the eyeball you can pull it forward and glue it into place. It won't shut again, but she'll look better."

It took ten minutes of cursing but the idea worked. Now one eye stayed open and the other shut when the doll was tipped backwards.

"Look, Maisie, she's winking at you."

Maisie giggled.

Tom mixed some grout and smoothed it into the cracks in the cheeks. "I'll paint the face later" he promised. "That's the best I can do."

"Po' Jem. Po' gir'," Maisie sighed, kissing the invalid.

Her mother stitched the head back onto the body and placed Jemima in her daughter's arms, urging her to be gentle because the glue wasn't properly hard. "Take her out on the verandah and sing her to sleep," she advised. "It's too hot to be cooped up in the house. You go out too, and read your paper, Tom. You've not had a chance this morning. I'm going to lie down on the bed for an hour."

It was a typical Saturday afternoon in Forrestville. Even the dog was dozing, except when a fly landed on his nose. Then Docker woke and snapped at it before putting his head down again on his paws.

An hour later Gruntfuttock and his bird returned from the footie and trashed the newly-planted petunias.

"That does it!" Tom threw the paper to one side and strode angrily towards Gruntfuttock's drive. Maisie followed, holding Jemima by one arm. "You're a lout!" Tom shouted. "You're an inconsiderate, fat-arsed, mean-minded bastard. Scum! That's what you are. Scum!"

"What did you say, arsehole?"

"I said you're scum. Even broke the kid's doll. Utter bastards, the pair of you!"

"Hit him, Grunt," said the moll. "Piss off, you old bugger!"

Gruntfuttock's meaty fist thwacked into Tom's gut. As he doubled over in pain an uppercut landed in the centre of his face, splitting his lip and bloodying his nose. Another blow caught him in the eye. Tom staggered and fell to his knees.

Maisie started screaming. Gruntfuttock snatched Jemima from her hand and put his great paw around the doll's head. He held it in front of Tom's face and slowly squeezed. The glue gave way under the pressure. It held the pieces together but only just. The dents were back. Jemima looked terrible.

"I'll crush your head like this if you come round whingeing again," the biker growled. "Nobody messes with me!"

"Here, brat! Take your bleedin' dolly and go away." The foxy lady spat on Tom, grabbed Jemima and threw her to Maisie, who was too uncoordinated to catch the cartwheeling toy.

She picked up the victim and ran to the house, shouting, "Mum, Da bwoke. Jem bwoke." Tom shuffled in, trying to staunch the bleeding. Pat cried as she took steak from the refrigerator and laid it on her husband's swollen cheek. "We're going to the police," she said firmly. "He's not getting away with this! I'll drive. Maisie, you stay here and put Jemima to bed. We'll fix her again later."

Pat helped her husband into the front seat of the car and drove it slowly out of the carport. "You'll be sorry," she shouted to Gruntfuttock, who was polishing the Harley. "I'll have the law on you. And I'll dob you in about the dope you smoke!"

Gruntfuttock threw a can of car polish at the battered old Holden. "Shite, Darl! Get the bong and the mull and make yourself scarce. Ain't got no speed left, have we? That bitch'll have the pigs round here, taking the place to pieces."

"Where'll I hide it?"

"Take the stuff across the road to the park. I'll meet you by the lake when I've got some more beer and a pizza. Fetch towels and your bikini. Get a nice tan while you wait."

Maisie, peering through the palings, watched the kerfuffle as the foxy lady gathered sunglasses and oil, and shoved a towel-wrapped bundle into the panniers at the back of the Harley. The moll dashed inside to change. She returned with a bottle of wine, which she clutched in her arms as she gingerly lowered herself onto the hot pillion seat. Gruntfuttock revved the engine and slowly rode the gleaming machine over the kerb and into the deserted park. Maisie locked Docker into the back garden and followed them down to the trees around the ornamental pond. It was a favourite spot on a hot day. The water was too shallow to be a danger and she often splashed there in summer.

Gruntfuttock was long gone, leaving only a vague smell of fuel on the air. It mingled with the scent of coconut oil that the moll had liberally spread over her nakedness, and the heavy; herbal odour of cannabis. The moll was enjoying a bong. The bottle of wine stood, unopened, by her side. Maisie watched from behind a bush as the woman rolled onto her back and lay, spread-eagled, on the towel, her eyes closed in ecstasy. She snored gently. She looked like Jemima, when Jemirna was asleep.

The hot anger inside Maisie could not be controlled. It continued to burn even after she'd taken off her clothes and rolled around in the cool water. She glanced about her and saw nobody. Gathering her discarded clothes, she walked with determination towards the sleeper and picked up the bottle of wine by the neck. Maisie was strong. The first blow smashed into the woman's temple. The second broke her nose and, with a mighty blow, Maisie swung at the jaw. That was better. The moll looked more like Jemima, now. Maisie, head on one side, considered the situation. It was still wrong. The foxy lady's eyes were in place, staring glassily at her. Maisie put the neck of the bottle against one and pushed hard. That was better. The eyeball was pushed to one side. The thing did not say, "Baby wanna wee-wee," but a pool of wetness gathered under her thighs.

The neck of the bottle was wet and yucky. In fact, the whole bottle was smeared with"stuff". Maisie wiped it clean with her knickers and stood it upright again. She took a second roll in the pond, got dressed and went home. Docker was glad to see her. He sniffed the stained knickers with interest but Maisie would not let him play with the meaty-smelling garment.

"Durdy," she explained.

The garden incinerator was still burning the dead tomato plants Tom had uprooted that morning. Maisie poked the garbage until it burst into flames again and thrust her knickers into the heart of the fire. She closed the lid and went into the kitchen to get a drink of cordial.

She was sitting on the verandah, nursing Jemima, when Pat and Tom returned, followed by a police car, which parked in Gruntfuttock's drive.

"He's not here," the constable shouted. "Did the kid see where he went?"

Maisie pointed. "Pa'k."

A few minutes later the men in blue returned, Gruntfuttock between them, handcuffed. "I didn't do it!" The biker was roaring wildly, protesting his innocence. "I found her like that!"

"You had the damned bottle in your hand," snarled the constable, red-faced from trying to control the struggling man. "Murderin' bastard!"

"What's happened?" Tom was wide-eyed.

"He's only beaten the moll to death. Horrible!"

"I'm innocent," Gruntfuttock screamed. "I'd been down the

bottle-shop. She was dead when I got back."

"Tell that to the magistrate," snapped the constable, pushing him into the back of the police car. "You're a vicious bastard, Malloy. What did she do? Steal your mull? You should have seen her, Mr Burman. Smashed her face to pieces."

"Doll bwoke," grunted Maisie, nodding with satisfaction. She put her thumb in her mouth and crooned a wordless lullaby to Jemima.

The Blue Rinse Set

'Curls' - the fashionable hair-stylists salon, had a prime position in the Benallan Shopping Centre. Aubrey Plum had secured a long lease, at favourable rental, from old Mr Ben Allan, who had been his bridge partner for years.

Ben Allan had ignored Mr Plum's discreet make-up, foppish clothes and girlish lisp. Such affectations did not detract from the man's acute card-sense. There was, after all, no scandal attached to his name. The only vice Mr Plum exhibited was his womanly taste for gossip. The only disagreement the friends ever had was when both went bald. Mr Allan polished his scalp; Mr Plum hid his under a silvery-blue wig, nicely waved.

Mr Allan had passed away the previous summer, leaving his entire estate to Mrs Elaine Truscott, his daughter. She was a regular customer and one who wanted control of every tenant in the shopping mall.

"I daren't offend her or she'll put up the rent of the salon," Mr Plum said, sighing. "I'm locked into an agreement for ten years to pay market value. Mr Allan was always reasonable. Elaine Truscott is not. I want to retire but she insists I fulfil my legal obligations. I'm sorry, Amber. You'll have to put up with her."

His assistant scowled. "I don't see why she always asks for me, when she always finds fault. Sadistic, she is. She won't let the other stylists touch that wire-brush she calls hair, yet she hates me doing it."

Mr Plum shrugged. "Just humour her, please."

"Easy for you to say. You're not the one she's nasty to. She makes me cringe, that she does."

"It's very odd. She was a pleasant enough girl," Monsieur

Plum remarked. "Then she got married."

"To Mr Truscott?" Amber looked up from the washbasin where she was noisily rinsing the thin curlers used for permanent waves. Her boss continued to clean his nails, glancing at them to ensure they were well-shaped. 'You like this colour, Amber? You don't think the rose-floss is too, too outrageous?'

His youngest assistant shook her head. "But you need a lip-gloss with less peach in it," she advised. "It doesn't suit your complexion. Who did the old cow marry then?"

"Her first mistake was a crook and a bully. By the time the Fraud Squad caught up with him, he'd embezzled more than two million dollars."

"Oo-er!"

"He skipped the country. Coughing up the missing funds turned Elaine really sour. Her second ran off with a cinema usherette. Had red hair, just like yours."

"You mean I remind her? That's daft! Anyway, Mr Truscott seems nice enough. He's a gentleman. I like cutting his hair."

"I've noticed. Pity he never says boo to his wife, dearie. She needs strong handling."

"With a barge pole, I reckon. I'm sorry for him."

"He speaks highly of you. Maybe that's what annoys Elaine. There's nothing going on between you, is there?"

"Here, what d'you think I am?" Amber tossed her curls and, rather flushed, flounced out of the back room. It was none of Mr Plum's business what she did in her free time. She was always careful with her after-hours customers. She provided a very special service and they respected her discretion. Even her fiance, Hubert, raised no objections to her visits to her middle-aged and geriatric clients. The appointments were sometimes in their own homes, when their wives were out; more often at their places of business, after other staff had left. In fact, Hubert often waited for her in the car outside while she performed her intimate specialty.

"It's a very private thing," she explained to Hubert. "I make them cry, you see. Men don't like other people to see them blubbing."

He kissed the tip of her nose. "Well, you're not doing it to me, that's all I'm going to say. As long as they pay well for the privilege."

"You know they do, Hubert. I've saved it all for when we move to our own place."

"I count the days, sweetheart. It'll be soon, I promise."

It wasn't soon enough.

Mrs Truscott complained bitterly after her next hair appointment, when she accused Amber of leaving her under the drier too long with the heat turned up to crisping point.

"You could have turned it down," Amber protested. "I gave you the heat controls."

"I fell asleep. You have a duty of care to make sure your customers don't nod off. My ears are quite sore."

"You had cotton wool pads over them, Mrs Truscott. Nobody else complains."

"I'm not everybody else. I have very sensitive skin. My scalp is burning."

"That's the rinse you insisted on. I warned you to stay with the henna-based hair-dye. It's much gentler."

"It's too red. You knew I wanted a bluer tint."

"And very nice it will look, too," said Amber, gritting her teeth as she took out the rollers. "I'll just brush it out for you."

Mrs Truscott sailed out fifteen minutes later, tight purplish curls lacquered in place. She'd demanded a discount for pain and suffering. Mr Plum had waived all charges. He was not pleased with Amber. He was even less pleased when, three days later, his nightmare client stormed in to the salon, protesting that the set had been a failure and almost all the curl had dropped out.

He fingered the limp tresses delicately. "It's too long, Mrs Truscott. You can't expect setting lotion to cope with the length of hair you have now. It's very heavy, you see. Thick and heavy. You need a cut and a thin, and a nice new permanent wave."

"Is that so? I'll have a proper blue rinse at the same time. When can you fit me in?"

Mr Plum looked at the appointment book. "Not until Friday, I'm afraid. Can you wait two days?"

"I'll have to, won't I? But you'll do me yourself, won't you? I don't trust Amber with the scissors."

"I'll style it for you, but you know I don't touch perms," he said, doubtfully. "It ruins my hands."

"Oh, let Miriam do the curlers. Amber'd mess that up, I expect. But you dress it out, Mr Plum."

"Of course, dear Madame. Are you coming to the bridge club tonight?"

"Looking like this? I think not. I shall wear a headscarf and go to the cinema. I want to see Brad Pitt in 'Troy'."

"Will Mr Truscott enjoy that?"

"Claude? No, I'll go alone. He has a meeting every Thursday nights. Freemasons or something"

Mrs Truscott made few mistakes in her life, other than her choice of men, but had not looked at the cinema program in the local paper. *Troy* was over. The film that night was the new Harry

Potter movie. Dismayed at not seeing rippling muscles and testosterone-charged violence, she thought of Clause. She would go home and prepare to seduce him.

There was a strange car parked outside her mansion. The owner appeared to be asleep, but as she turned into the drive she could hear the boom boom of loud music and see the man's head nodding gently to the beat. She shouted to him to turn the volume down but he had headphones on and was quite oblivious to external sound.

Seething with annoyance, she let herself into the house and went quickly up the stairs to take off her outdoor clothes. There was a light on in the room Claude used as a study. She pushed the door open and screamed.

Claude Truscott, in his silk dressing gown, was lying back on a recliner armchair, his face in the glare of a bright lamp. On his lap, astride his legs, was Amber, her face close to his as she performed her specialty. With a roar, the angry wife grabbed Amber by the back of her blouse and threw her onto the floor. Clause, pulling the lever to make the recliner spring upright, struggled to his feet, only to be knocked back into the seat by a mighty blow to the face.

"Elaine," he yelled, trying to stand, pressing a towel to his nose to stop the bleeding. "You don't understand…"

She slapped him down again. "You and that slut! Get out, Get out, you wicked girl! Get out before I kill you!"

Amber, staring aghast at the wrathful Mrs Truscott, pulled her skirt straight and ran from the room and out of the house. She got into the car and shook her fiance.

"Hubert! Wake up, you dozy bugger. Get me out of here!"

He drove like Formula One to their apartment. When they were safe inside and she told him what had happened, he disappointed her by falling into fits of helpless laughter.

"It's not funny," said Amber. "She was giving him a tremendous beating."

"She thought...she must have thought..." Hubert howled again. "And I don't suppose he paid you first."

"Of course he didn't. I hadn't finished him off!" Amber, suddenly seeing the funny side herself, collapsed into Hubert's arms. "Oh, dear. And she's coming in for an appointment tomorrow. Thank goodness you've sorted out the other business."

"Have you told old Plum you're leaving?"

She shook her head. "We're short-handed, you see. He's already tearing his hair out...well, he would be if he had any!"

They were more than short-handed on Friday morning. Miriam and Michelle, the other stylists, both rang to say they had gastric flu. Genevieve, the apprentice, came in looking rather green and spent the next fifteen minutes retching into the hair-washing bowl. Mr Plum sent her home in a taxi.

"That leaves you and me," he said, gloomily.

"Don't you think it's time you retired, Mr Plum? You shouldn't have to put up with all this worry"

"I know, I know. And my widowed sister keeps asking me live with her on the Gold Coast. I'm tempted. But Mrs Truscott's got me over a barrel, dearie. You know how it is."

"Would you be pleased if she was out of your life? Wouldn't that be smashing?"

"Blissful, dearie, but let's get through today, shall we? I'll cut and set, but you'll have to do the dragon's perm."

"She won't like that. You see, there's been a bit of trouble with her over Mr Truscott. I was doing him a favour and she caught us in the act."

"Oh, Amber. What have you done?"

"If he wants you to know, he can tell you himself! He's just parked outside and is heading this way."

"Perhaps his wife's cancelled," said Mr Plum, hopefully.

The salon door opened. Claude Truscott came in, wearing sunglasses. When he saw there was no one else around, he took them off. He had two black eyes and a very swollen nose. There was a bruise on his jaw and a plaster on his cheek.

"Oh, dearie. You have been in the wars," Mr Plum said. "Have you been mugged?"

Claude hung his head. "Sort of," he admitted. "I just dropped in to pay Amber what I owe her. And to give her back her things. She left in a hurry last night." He laid a leather roll on the counter. "I'm sorry about the trouble, young lady. I've put a little extra in the envelope as compensation."

Mr Plum probed delicately for an explanation, but Mr Truscott fobbed him off.

"I don't want to talk about it, Aubrey. You're such a gossip that I'd be the laughing stock of the town. But don't blame Amber, she's a good girl." He left through the back door, which led into the Benallan Mall, where he had his office, thus avoiding the first hairdressing clients, who were entering from the car park.

The next hours passed in a frenzy. Scissors flashed like lightning and hair piled up around Mr Plum's feet. Amber's fingers wound hair onto rollers and twirled the brushes for blow-waves. Clients came in like dags and went out like models. Elaine Truscott arrived at 11am and sat in the waiting room, flicking through magazines and
muttering about the delay.

"It's not good enough," she snapped when finally seated before the big mirror. "I expect preferential treatment, Mr Plum.

How can you expect to run a proper salon without enough staff? Sheer incompetence. Your girls have no business getting sick."

Amber, washing the hair of the butcher's wife in the side room, pursed her lips. The woman was a brute. She was being so nasty to Mr Plum, threatening to double the rent, being a real bitch. Poor Claude, having to live with a vicious harridan like that! He was a proper gentleman, even at the most intimate moments.

She glanced through the gap in the curtain, noting the worried frown on the brow beneath the silver-blue hair of Mr Plum. His lips and cheeks were tinged the same shade. "She'll give him a heart attack if she doesn't leave off," she muttered, pouring conditioner onto her client's scalp and massaging it in.

"And you must sack Amber," Mrs Truscott ordered. "I won't have that girl working in my shopping centre. Sack her at once!"

"I can't do that. She's entitled to a fortnight's notice."

"Nonsense. Give her two week's pay in lieu."

"No," said Mr Plum. "I can't afford it."

"I'll give you the money," snarled the nightmare on legs. "Just get rid of her."

"But there's only her and me! She'll have to do your perm. I don't touch the lotion, you know that."

"Then immediately afterward, you hear me?"

Mr Plum looked shaken as he escorted Mrs Truscott to the washbasins, where he donned rubber gloves and applied the blue rinse she demanded.

"I must warn you that it may not agree with the perming chemicals." he twittered.

"Nonsense, it wouldn't dare defy my wishes," the dragon hissed. "Get on with it, man!"

Amber took her client to the styling station. The butcher's wife was soon pinned into rollers and settled under the drying hood with a copy of Cosmopolitan. Amber slipped out of the salon to fetch her a cappuccino from the cafe next door. She made a quick detour into the pharmacy before returning with the froth-topped drink. Then she went into the cubicle where the perming trolley was stored and made sure she had the usual permanent wave lotion, plenty of cotton wool and rollers of the right size. She poured the solution into a bowl and stirred it around with her special additive. The pungent smell filled the air as she wheeled the trolley next to her victim.

Elaine Truscott glared at her while Amber combed the liquid through her hair, wincing as the young stylist pulled out wet strands and wound them as tightly as possible onto perming rods. She complained bitterly as each little sausage was soaked in extra liquid and cotton wool slipped between them. Amber ignored her griping and tied the mesh scarf over her head, encasing the whole in a plastic hood.

Mr Plum gave a final spray to the curls of the butcher's wife and took a deep breath. There were no other customers. He beckoned Amber into his office and gave her the bad news. "I'm sorry," he said, counting out two week's money. "You heard her. If I don't dismiss you, I'll be in financial trouble. Go now, dearie. I'll wash her out."

"That's fine by me," Amber said, suppressing a grin. She took her coat and handbag and went out through the back door into the mall. She glanced at her watch. The fun was about to start. She knocked on the door of Truscott and Bailey Accountants. "Have you finished up here, Claude? Come on. Join me for coffee. We'll get a table where we can see into Curls. You'll like this." She smiled at the perfect gentleman. "Mr Plum is just about to unwind your wife's perm."

The plastic hood came off then the tonsorial artist untied

the mesh scarf. Amber watched with glee as every rod on Mrs Truscott's head fell to the floor around her. The rods were bare and, apart from a blue-scum, so was Elaine Truscott's scalp. The dragon screamed as her bald reflection stared back at her.

Claude gasped for breath and his eyes were out on stalks. "Kee-rist, Amber. What have you done? How did you manage that?"

"Mixed hair-removing gel with the perming stuff," she grinned.

Other coffee-drinkers gathered round to find the cause of the hullabaloo in Curls. Mrs Truscott had pulled Mr Plum's pants down was leathering his backside with a hairbrush. 'I'll sue you, you stinking little ponce," she bellowed, casting him to one side. She rubbed the gunge off her scalp with a towel, snatched the silver-blue wig from Mr Plum's head and pulled it over her own. She raced out like an advancing tornado.

"Dear lord," spluttered Claude, into his coffee "What does she look like?"

The salon door slammed. Mr Plum stalked out and threw the keys on the table in front of Mr Truscott. "You can tell your wife she can do what the hell she likes with Curls," he said. "I'm walking out on her."

"Tell her yourself," said Claude. "I'm doing the same thing. I'm going into partnership with Hubert and Amber. We've leased premises in Parramatta to exploit her special talents. I'll do the books and drum up business; Hubert will barber and shave clients"

"Look, Mr Plum. I've got the first brochures ready." Amber pulled the leather roll from her handbag and opened it. Inside were magnifying spectacles with a tiny torch attached, dentists' mirrors, soft-tipped tweezers and a tube of the numbing gel mothers use on teething babies. She passed a glossy pamphlet to her former employer. It said:

Wombat
For The Hairy-Nosed
Get Plucked With Compassion

And It Came To Pass

And it came to pass, in the Year of the Lord, that Man's days were numbered.

Judgement: Chapter Two: Verse 12.

We could see the man approaching when he was still more than a kilometre away, walking out of the dust along the road to Woomera. There was a shimmering heat haze on the horizon and he came as if from nowhere, out of the Australian desert, out of the sun, as brown and sere as if he were part of the Dreamtime. At first he was no more than a stick figure, like a man from a Drysdale painting, long and thin. As he grew nearer we could see he was wearing a flowing robe, like a kaftan, common enough among the protesters who gathered outside the gates of the Detention Centre, and even more usual amongst the detainees, most of whom were asylum seekers from the Middle East. He had a long beard, thin and brown, like the hair which curled over his shoulders. He had sandals on his feet and carried a rough staff with a notch in the end for the thumb, such as is popular with those who are accustomed to walk in the mountains.

There was usually a buzz of morning chatter among the television and newspaper crews gathered at the gates, keeping an eye on the encampments of protest groups, which had become part of life outside a news hot-spot. They had been gathering energy for the daily ritual of placards and chanting, performed as soon as the sun had warmed their blood to the point of activity. The desert nights are cold. They warmed themselves with coffee and freedom songs, but even those trailed off as the man got closer. They joined us near the gates and fell silent.

The man's face was brown and beautiful, not handsome, but

cast with lines which come through suffering, overlain by the patina of peace and acceptance. His shoulders were bowed, as if from carrying a heavy burden, yet he walked tall and easy, his steps firm and sure. His smile was kind and his eyes shone with an inner light. He did not speak as he passed us.

The guards swung open the gates to let him through. They did not ask for his papers or search him for weapons. They simply let him pass. They made no move to stop us following, so we did, quietly, as if drawn to the man's footsteps, but at a distance to show our respect.

He did not speak, but the children came to him, laughing and dancing. Mothers carried their babies from the huts and placed them in his arms. Those he could not carry he kissed and passed to older children, who received them willingly. Then he raised a hand in farewell and walked on, out into the desert, through the fences on the far side of the camp, and into the morning mirage. And the children went with him.

We watched until they were gone. No one lifted a finger to stop him.

When the trance was broken, for trance it must have been, guards sounded alarms, drove us out of the camp and slammed the gates shut. From inside the huts rose a great communal wailing, a sobbing of sorrow and an ululation of emptiness, interspersed with cries of anguish and anger. It broke in waves which sent shivers through us.

"The children have gone!"

Correspondents raised base and sent the headline news across the world. There was no camera footage. The crews wilted under a bollocking from their producers, who wanted, one and all, to know if they had been paralysed or were just plain stupid. I got through to my news room.

"Is this some sort of a stunt?" my editor snapped. "The same thing's just been called in from Curtin Detention Centre and Port Hedland. Same guy, same modus operandi, same time."

"That's impossible," I gasped. "Must have been a look-alike."

"Well-planned operation, whoever did it."

"Al-Qaeda?" I asked.

"Beats me. But whoever's behind it, the question is, where are they taking the kids? They must have aircraft standing by to fly them out. Any sign of aircraft where you are?"

"Only the police helicopter. And some RAAF jets which seem to be doing a systematic search of the area."

"I'm sending our chopper for you. Get back to base, Jackson. Leave young Markham to get the follow-up story out there. There are reports coming in like you'd never believe."

*

Entering our Australian office was like entering bedlam. Phones ringing, men shouting, women crying, a bank of television consoles screening live footage or playing background music from a dozen different countries. There was pandemonium and, behind the superficial noise, the dull drumbeat of a global uproar.

"He's taken out Christmas Island!" yelled a reporter, with the phone still pressed to his ear. "No sign of a ship off-shore!"

The Man, and his clones, had walked through the refugee camps of Afghanistan and Pakistan, through the war-ravaged streets of Palestine and Israel, through the hordes of Indians and Kashmiris fleeing the threat of nuclear disaster in the Himalayan foothills. They had been seen in the wastelands of Cambodia and along the Thai border. They had walked among the shell-holes of Chechnya and the ruins of Bosnia, Croatia and Albania. The shanty towns of South Africa were shell-shocked. Sudanese children had walked away from slavery.

"What is going on?" screamed the editor.

"God knows. Reports are just coming in from Somalia and Angola. What's the position in Europe?"

"War zones first, apparently. Detention Centres next. Then refugee camps."

"I've got Bangkok on the line! The Man's in the red light area, rounding up the young prostitutes. Shall I call the Philippines, see what goes down there?"

"Do that. Just do that!"

"United Nations is calling crisis talks. The President's going on air at 1600 Washington time."

"What's our Prime Minister saying?"

"'No Comment.' He's talking to the Immigration Minister."

"The Man's not on his own any more," said a Shanghai stringer. "He's got this fat, bald monk wearing yellow robes walking with him through the slave labour camps in China."

"Did someone report there's a mullah with him in Kabul?" asked the editor.

"Yeah, with a whole string of camels. Reports from Africa suggest the Man's playing havoc in Zimbabwe now. Cleared the Congo at daybreak."

"Go on, someone say it. We don't know who they are but they all look the same to us!"

"Clones. They've got to be clones!"

"Anybody tried to take him out yet?"

"Some nutters in Rio. Seems the authorities were pretty pleased to see the street kids go, but the Man's just rounded up a couple of regular schools. All gone! Tempers are getting pretty thin over there. There's been gunfire but they can't touch him. He just walks on, smiling, and the children follow him."

"Follow him where?"

"God knows. Into thin air, it seems. One minute they're there, the next, they've vanished."

I looked from one screen to another, several showing the Man leading crowds of children. I knew that face. Africa, America, Asia, yet I knew that face. It was one face that was unforgettable. I felt a huge surge of recognition and a bubble of exultation and dread burst from me. "Jesus Christ!" I shouted. "That's the Man! He's taking them home."

"What's that you say, Jackson? Who's taking them where?"

"Suffer little children to come unto me, for theirs is the Kingdom of Heaven. The Man is the Nazarene."

My editor goggled. "Crap!" he said. "More likely to be an Alien Conspiracy."

"Get this, then, on CNN." I pointed to the screen carrying live vision from Baltimore.

The reporter was crying as she spoke, describing the scene at a local remand centre where the inmates had just been released. "We've just come away from the children's home for the handicapped; the nurse said the patients left half-an-hour ago. They were all walking, even the kids with spina bifida and the poor little mites who were bedridden. The kids with crutches threw them away and ran off with the Man. Look, there are miracles happening all around us. I don't know what's going on, but there ain't no unhappy faces among the ones who've been called. Over to you in Alabama."

The screen showed a dirt road and a shanty town on the wrong side of the tracks. You could see the Man coming, a crowd of youngsters at his heels and a tall, dark man at his side. "That's

Martin Luther King," said the editor. "But it can't be."

You could see the crowd getting closer, a hundred or more, black and white, laughing and singing. As they drew close to the cameras, interference filled the screen. We could hear the crews cursing as they tried to swing round for a view of the departure.

"They came right up with us," cried the reporter. "The Man just smiled and, as they passed, they all disappeared. It's incredible!"

Our editor sighed so deeply you'd have thought he was breathing through his backside. "Okay, Jackson. Suppose you're right. Suppose the damned Nazarene is taking them home. Why's he, and I suppose I'd better start giving that a capital letter, why's He taking the Muslims and the Buddhists and the effing Communists, huh?"

"In my Father's house there are many mansions. I go to prepare a place for them or something like that. Isn't that the way the Bible tells it?"

"You mean we've had two thousand years of hands-off and suddenly He decides to call off the deal?"

"Something like that. He and Mohammad and Buddha and Shiva and the rest of the Hindu Gods. The Theists have always argued there is only one Omnipotent in a variety of manifestations."

"I thought that was Theosophists?" The editor was thumbing through his dictionary. "No, you're right. The one's I'm thinking of are into the occult and mysticism. Supernatural powers and the like."

"You don't call this supernatural?" I could only shake my head. Strange how civilised men liked to put little boxes around philosophies and concepts they couldn't understand.

"You reckon Papa Doc will go along with this, down in Haiti? Voodoo country?" he asked me.

"I expect the Man cleared that place out first."

"Okay. So he's taking the poor and the hungry and the sick and the lame. Where's it going to stop?"

"Maybe it isn't."

"Isn't what?"

"Going to stop. Maybe the Man's working on a triage system, taking the emergency cases first."

"Shit! You got kids, Jackson? Go home and be with them."

"Hey, come on, boss. What's the United Nations going to do? Come on, switch channels. Let's hear what's going down."

"Go home, I said. Look, what do you think the United Nations can do if it's as you suggest? Negotiate a deal? Pay an effing ransom? Start a global prayer session? Build a hundred effing pyramids or sacrifice a million effing sheep? Go home!"

I realised he was crying. No sobbing or anything ostentatious. Just tears, big fat tears. "You've got grandchildren," I reminded him.

"Good kids," he said. "I've enjoyed them. I'll phone them tonight. Not to say goodbye, or anything. I wouldn't want to frighten them. Just to tell them we love them, just in case they get the call."

By the time I left there was just a skeleton crew on duty. The boss sent everyone home who had children of school age or younger. My wife looked at me gravely as I came into the house. She'd been crying but was putting a brave face on it.

"Where are the kids?" I asked, when I could shake off her embrace..

"They're upstairs, playing Harry Potter games on the DVD. I've not let them watch television."

"You know, though."

"Yes. I know."

"Dear God, how could this be happening to us?"

"Maybe if we'd done a bit more, Dear God, and meant it, it wouldn't have," she replied.

"Too late for that now, darling." I hugged her. "I think I'll go and play the computer too. Tomorrow we'll fly back to the States to see the grandparents. I've bought tickets."

She smiled through her tears. "Let us now go even unto Disneyland and see this thing which has come to pass."

*

It took two weeks for the last of the children to be called. There had been a certain amount of complacency when the exodus involved the outcasts of society. The world was overpopulated, said the pundits. We were seeing, they blathered, a kind of natural selection, an evolution of the species. There was outrage when the Man came for the children of the idle rich, the young athletes, the sons and daughters of celebrities. Lock them in a lead-lined bomb-shelter for safety and the most loved and protected child seemed to vaporise. The call was universal. Yeah, even unto Disneyland!

We had ten days of happy companionship with ours before they left. The Amish communities were among the last to be gathered in by the Nazarene.

Then there was nothing. The Man and the Man's Men no longer walked the Earth.

Soldiers laid down their arms and went home to mourn. Churches were full. Mosques overflowed. Temples and Synagogues shook to the devotions of the faithful. The human race went down on its knees and begged forgiveness. It was not to be.

It was months before the grim reality dawned on us. There were no babies. Those who had been carrying at the time of the Great Passing, gave birth only to the stillborn. Early foetuses were miscarried or reabsorbed. Those with fertilised embryos, frozen ready for implantation, found technology futile. There were no babies that year, the Year of The Lord, nor have there been any since.

We are a dying race.

It is twenty years since the Great Passing and in that time there have been no wars. There has been no famine, for we are faster to help and kinder to our fellow men. There have been no disputes over national boundaries, for negotiation has achieved what terror could not. The power mad have been humbled, the crooked have gone straight, the perverts have been scared into conformity.

We eat well, sleep deep, work hard to dull the knowledge that there is nothing worth working for. Our youngest citizens are thirty-five. In another ten years there will be no woman on this planet capable of bearing a child, even if a miracle were to happen and fertility were to be given us again as a Blessing.

In sixty years time the planet will no longer feel the footsteps of Homo Sapiens. Forests will regenerate and buildings will crumble. The animal kingdom will take our place and, who knows, maybe the great apes will come into their own. Or maybe rats will rule the land. The seas will not be contaminated by our pollution and the air will be free from our industrial waste. You can feel the tempo of our lives slowing and the beat of Mankind's pulse weakening.

I am kept busy, writing the last book of the Bible, Judgement. Who knows if there will ever be another sentient race to read my poor attempts to emulate the Gospel Makers?

My prayer, and my unspoken hope, is that one day the Man will look down upon our planet, and see it reborn to the beauty with which the Creator endowed it. Then, maybe, the Nazarene will relent and, smiling, will lead some of our children home, to a new world.

But I know in my heart that this really is

The End.